WONDERMENT

A STEEL ROSES NOVEL

B.L.WILDE

*For Nick, who made me believe in myself again. I'm not
sure I could have continued writing without you.*

CONTENTS

A STEEL ROSES NOVEL

A STEEL ROSES NOVEL

WONDERMENT

B.L.Wilde

"Steel Roses is like a religion, and on that stage I'm a fucking god!"

Alex Harbour 2020

WONDERMENT

PROLOGUE

T he beat of the drums pounded in my chest. From the side of the stage, the screaming was deafening. Steel Roses fans had waited so long for this moment. I could hardly believe I was
right here beside Alex as he took his first step back into the limelight that had destroyed him all those years ago. He was clutching his legendary guitar, waiting for his cue.

"You'll be fine," I whispered into his ear.

"Have you *heard* that crowd?" He tried to laugh it off but swallowed nervously. "I used to think I was born for this, but it fucked me up so bad the first time around. Do I really want to do this again?"

"You didn't have me standing by you last time." The worry in his eyes faded as he pulled me towards him. My body crashed painfully against his guitar, but I didn't care once his lips pressed softly to mine.

"Don't move from this spot, Straight Lace. I need to be able to see you while I'm on stage," he muttered, leaning back to look at me.

"I'm not going anywhere. I'll be right here."

With a smile on his face, he finally let me go and moved to take his place on centerstage. The audience went wild as a single spotlight fell on Alex. My heart whimpered at the sight. How *was* I going to protect him from the hysteria that surrounded him this time around?

CHAPTER ONE

"**B**aby Cakes, did you steal my hair straighteners again?" Diego frowned as he wandered into my office in silver hot pants and a crop top. Only he could pull off that look.

I'd been back in LA for over a month. Alex and I had been practically inseparable since he had declared that he was falling for me on my birthday. Though it had been nearly impossible to get him to attend without me, he was currently at a lunch meeting with Gina. There was a lot for me to organize with the Steel Roses reunion, and I needed space to sort it all out. Alex was finally starting to understand that.

"I didn't have them last time," I snorted, spinning in my chair to face him. "What do you *really* want?"

"To gossip...like always." He threw his long blonde hair over his shoulders as he perched his perfect butt on my desk. Diego was seriously the most feminine person I knew and I adored him for it. "Has Alex told you when he's meeting up with all the guys yet?"

"No. It seems Matt keeps putting it off, though." I could hardly believe that the biggest rock band in the world was getting back together. The very band I'd been obsessed with as a teenager...and now I was *dating* the lead singer!

"Stubborn fucker!" Diego muttered under his breath. "Alex is handling this better than I thought, though. You are such a blessing for him."

"I'm not doing much, really." The truth was, we'd spent most of the month in bed, not that I was complaining.

"Nat, you're the one that put him back together again. Surely you must see that? His new album went *Platinum* and it was *all* about you!"

"Not *all* the songs were about me," I protested. Diego gave me his '*Bitch, please*' glare before I had even finished. "They weren't! Alex told me so himself."

"You really need to realize what you mean to him, Baby Cakes." With a roll of my eyes, I looked towards the double doors leading out to the pool area. Alex was leaning against the frame, looking more godly than was humanly possible. His ripped jeans hung low off his hips and his fitted white shirt clung to his well-defined chest. He'd been working out more regularly these days, knowing that a world tour was on the horizon. I was such a lucky bitch.

"What are you two gossiping about now?" he chuckled, making a beeline for me.

"I'm trying to find out if you're going to put extra padding in your boxers when you're on tour," Diego teased. He turned to wink at me as Alex leaned down and kissed my lips.

"You know I don't wear boxers on stage, fucker, and Nat wouldn't tell you shit like that. My girl has my back." His girl? Gah! I still melted when he said it, and he'd been calling me that for weeks now.

"Oh, do you remember the time we stuffed your crotch with that tie dye shirt and you ended up with a red and blue..." Alex didn't give Diego a chance to finish.

"Yes, I remember," he snapped. "Don't you have somewhere you need to be?"

"Nope. I was planning on staying here and annoying you and Nat, actually. Don't you want to talk about your dyed junk?" Judging by the look on Alex's face, I knew this conversation was only going to end one way.

"Fuck off, Diego!" It amazed me how well I knew my rocker already. "I need a private word with Nat anyway."

"Oh, a *word*. Is *that* what you're calling it these days?" Alex and I must have both glared at Diego at the same time. "Jesus! Okay, I'm going! Stop with the death glares."

"One day he'll take offence at the way you speak to him," I said giggling. Once Diego was gone, I looked up at Alex and smiled.

"The insults are a compliment, really. He knows that." Running his hand through his short, freshly cut hair, he sighed. "Matt has called off the meeting again."

"What? Why? I thought he wanted this?" I'd gathered there was bad blood between Matt and Alex, but how were they ever going to get over their issues if they didn't even talk about them? "I know you're not ready to go into detail about you and the band, but is it really that bad?"

"Straight Lace, if you'd known me back then...you wouldn't have fallen for me."

"But I did fall for you. I was a groupie, remember? Anyway, I would have been under age. You should be thankful that you met me now instead," I teased.

"Oh, Baby, I'm thankful for you every day." Taking my hand, he pulled me up out of my chair so he could wrap his arms around me. "I'm not just thankful for this either." He ran his hands down my body before cupping my ass. "I'm just as thankful for your mind, your fiery temper, and your whimpers when you're about to cum."

"You are such a born romantic," I snorted, standing on my tiptoes to kiss him softly. Inside, I was burning for him. I loved the way he made me whimper, too.

"I'm trying," he groaned against my mouth, pulling on my bottom lip with his teeth. "Can I fuck you over your desk right now?"

"No!" I giggled at his attempt at romance. "I have work to do and the door is wide open."

"I could shut the door," he offered. It was hard to resist him when he was this playful, but I managed somehow.

"You had your wicked way with me earlier."

"It's never enough. You know that." His fingers tried to slip inside my shorts but I pulled away.

"Save it for later. Your personal trainer will be here in ten minutes."

"You know my schedule better than me."

"That's my job," I grinned. "Among other things."

"*Other things*? Is that what you're calling us now?" His clear blue eyes were laced with humor. "You wound me, Straight Lace."

"I'll make it up to you later. Now go!" He finally got the hint, and after a quick peck on the cheek, he was gone.

The news of Steel Roses reforming hadn't gone public yet. Of course, there were rumors of it everywhere. The paparazzi were constantly camped outside the Hollywood house and hounded Alex wherever he went. Shane had to hire a few extra guys for security, and all of it was because of gossip. I was trying really hard not to think about the madness that would envelop Alex once everything had been finalized.

Steel Roses fans were much older now. Surely that meant they would be mature and respectable towards the band. Right? When I thought about Liv and the fit she had when I told her that Alex and I were secretly dating, I sighed. Who was I kidding? The fans were going to be just as crazy now, if not worse.

At least Liv was talking to me again. Alex had even said that she could come and stay at the mansion, but I wasn't ready to watch my best friend drool all over my boyfriend yet. Especially since he looked unbelievably delicious. It was partly due to the work he'd been putting in with his personal trainer, but I hoped deep down some of it was because of me, too. Alex was happy for the first time in a long time. Everyone had noticed that.

Only Liv, Gina, Mary, Diego, Shane, and my parents knew about our relationship. Alex and I didn't want to draw attention to ourselves, so we kept our affection for each other behind closed doors. Because I was still his personal assistant, no one questioned when I moved back into his house in Hollywood Hills. I hadn't done very many events with him in the public eye yet, but I wasn't worried. We knew what we were doing. Besides, I agreed with him on one thing—it was a good idea to keep our relationship private until all the Steel Roses hype died down.

My parents were off on their travels again, touring around Australia. I was happy about that because it stopped my mother from fussing about me. To say that she was excited about my relationship with Alex was an understatement. She was already thinking about the wedding and would constantly bring it up. I kept telling her she was being ridiculous, though. I wasn't even sure if Alex was the marrying type.

After I'd finished replying to my emails, I decided to take a break. All of the media pages needed to be checked today which was always a big job, so I knew I'd need a rest.

Mary was busy humming along to the radio in the kitchen, but gave me a warm smile when she noticed me walk in.

"Vince is giving Alex quite the workout outside." She laughed and motioned towards the pool area where Alex was doing circuits around the pool.

"How can they work out in that heat? You'd think they'd use the air conditioned studio instead."

"I think Vince is punishing him for something." Vince *was* a tough trainer, but Alex needed that. "Why don't you take some water out to them?" Like I needed an excuse to go and perv at my shirtless boyfriend. At least I was making myself useful while doing it this time.

Grabbing a few bottles of ice-cold water, I made my way out towards the pool area. The heat was blistering, partly because there wasn't a cloud in the sky. It amazed me at how easily I'd gotten used to living back in LA. I didn't even miss the rain much anymore.

"There she is. My lifesaver." Alex panted breathlessly as he took a bottle of water from me. Vince didn't get the hidden meaning like I did. He didn't know we were dating, after all.

"You were looking a little hot. Mary thought you'd need a drink to cool down." I smiled sweetly as I tried to keep my eyes away from the beads of sweat that were trickling down his perfect chest. I'd become so accustomed to his body that it was difficult fighting the urge to touch him. "How are you doing, Vince?" I asked, taking my eyes off of Alex before I combusted.

"Good thanks, Nat. Taking Alex through his paces, as usual. You should join the workout next time. I'd enjoy putting you through your paces."

"Nat doesn't like brutal workouts." Alex glared at Vince, clenching his jaw. "She uses the gym in her free time anyway. She also doesn't need you coming on to her, fucker!" When would he learn to relax?

"I don't think he was coming onto me, Alex." I tried to laugh it off. "Were you, Vince?"

"No. I was just thinking the two of you could have done a circuit together. Jeez, man. I wouldn't hit on your PA. You know I'm professional and shit." Alex nodded apologetically at him but couldn't seem to meet with my concerned eyes. "Why don't we do a few more rounds on the punch bag? I don't think you've let off enough steam yet."

"Yeah, sorry man. I've got a lot on my mind." I wanted to reach out and hug him, but knew I'd have to wait until we were alone later. He'd been on edge about meeting up properly with the band all week, and the fact that Matt kept putting it off only made it worse.

"Come on, let's hit the bags." Vince patted him on the back. Alex gave me an apologetic smile as I turned to walk away.

"Has Alex finished his work out yet?" Shane asked as he walked into my office. I'd only just sat down. "What's up?" he asked in concern when he saw my face.

"It's nothing," I sighed, gazing down at my desk.

"Oh, don't start that bullshit. What has Alex done this

time?"

"Nothing. Matt wouldn't meet up with him again, that's all."

"Seriously? That's not a good start, is it? What excuse did he give this time?"

"I don't think he's ready to talk yet and it's playing on Alex's mind. They need to have this conversation if they're ever going to make this world tour work though."

"This tour is going to be a disaster no matter what. Diego has already said that I'll be breaking up more fights between the band than actually protecting them from their fans."

"I'm sure he was teasing." Deep down, I had a feeling Diego was telling the truth. Not liking where the conversation was heading, however, I changed the subject. "I'm glad Gina decided to use you for the overall security of the band."

"Naomi had more to do with it than Gina."

"Naomi?" I asked, confused. I hadn't heard that name before.

"The tour manager. She was with them the first time around." Oh, Alex had mentioned her now that I thought about it. "Diego has some funny stories about her. She seems like a laugh."

"I remember Alex telling me about her now. She's meant to be meeting with the band next month."

"Let's hope Matt will finally grow some balls by then," Shane teased just as one of his men called him. "Don't forget, it's your turn to pick the takeout tonight." Friday night was takeaway night with Alex, Diego and Shane. I had to admit, it was one of my favorite nights of the week. Last week we'd even gotten the karaoke machine out. Now *that* was an evening

I wouldn't forget any time soon. Listening to Diego and Alex dueting to Endless Love—I hadn't cried with laughter like that in a long time.

Once I'd gotten caught up on Alex's social media sites, the afternoon flew by. To say that his fanbase was crazy would have been an understatement. I'd declined over five thousand marriage proposals this week alone, and I didn't even want to *think* about the number of indecent photos I'd had to delete from his news feed. Most were fully grown women, but there were even some men, too. I had come across a few charity messages that I would talk to him about though. He liked to please the fans that deserved his time.

Takeaway evening had already begun when I wandered into the spacious living area. Alex was already stretched out on one of his red leather couches, playing the PlayStation with Shane. There were loads of chocolate wrappers scattered on the floor. Alex and his cadbury obsession. I'd need to order some more. We were already out of maltesers.

Diego was sitting sipping a glass of red wine, reading a gossip magazine. "About time. Where have you been?" He glanced up at me and sighed. "I'm so hungry I was thinking about eating my own arm."

I snorted. "Some of us have to work you know." Alex had thrown his game controller down and was holding his arms open for me as I made my way over to him.

"Your boss sounds like a real slave driver. Why do you put up with his shit?" Alex grinned as I fell into his arms and straddled his lap.

"I'm not sure. Maybe it's because I'm crazy about him."

"Crazy you say?" he whispered, his lips brushing his lips

against mine as he spoke. "I think he's pretty *crazy* about you, too."

"If you two are planning on fucking on that couch anytime soon, can you let Shane and me know? I'm not in the mood for live porn tonight." Alex and I both turned towards a smug looking Diego. Pecking Alex's lips, I reluctantly moved off him so we could order the takeaway.

"How about pizza?" I asked, looking through the leaflets. "I'll order a mixture. Do we want to pick up or have them delivered?"

"I can order and grab them. I need to get some more beer anyway." Shane stood up and patted his jeans for his wallet.

"You're leaving me with Mr. and Mrs. Gropey?" Diego pouted. "Fuck that. I'll come with you to get them. I can eat some chicken wings on the way back so I don't start gnawing off my arm."

"We love you, too," Alex called out at Diego as he and Shane left.

"Mr. and Mrs. Gropey was pretty funny," I giggled, crawling back on top of him. My hands began to wander up his top, feeling his well-toned abs under my fingertips. His breathing started to come out in gasps as I moved lower, running my hands over the bulge in his jeans.

"If you're only going to tease me, Straight Lace, you need to fucking stop right now. My cock can only take so much."

"When do I *ever* tease you?" Batting my eyelashes at him, I slowly undid his zip. "We have at least thirty minutes until they get back anyway."

"Thirty minutes?" Before I could blink, I was pinned underneath him. "Let's skip the oral then. I just want to bury my

17

cock inside you." His words always made me instantly wet. His hands began to gently pull my shorts down, and all I could do was groan into his mouth when his lips crashed against mine. His fingers stroked me softly, testing to see if I was ready. "Fuck, I love that you get turned on so easily. You're always ready for me."

"That's because I always want you," I yearned, rubbing my sex against him. He took that as an invitation, and within moments, his jeans were halfway down his legs and he was pushing deeply inside me.

"This is going to be fast, Baby," he groaned, setting a maddening pace. He gripped my legs and lifted me slightly off the couch as he pushed deeper inside me. "You like that, huh?" he smirked, watching my face.

"Shit! You know I do." I was already beginning to climb, and I knew this wouldn't be the only climax I had in the next half an hour.

I was such a lucky bitch!

CHAPTER TWO

"Once everything has been finalized with Rock Records and the band, I'll be able to send over Alex's new schedule. Is he still off the drink?" Gina had hardly looked up at me during our meeting.

"Yes."

"And the drugs? Are you sure he's not on anything?"

"I'm sure, Gina. He's completely clean. I think he'd even let you do a drug test if you're that worried."

"No, I'll take your word for it. You know him better than anyone these days."

"And you're okay with that? The fact that I know him *that* well?" I'd been meaning to have a chat about Alex and I dating, but Gina and I were so rarely alone.

"What do you mean, Nat?" She smirked, looking up at me.

"Well, you gave me this job, and I'm worried that you think I've somehow undermined you."

"Why would you think that?"

"I'm Alex's PA, and..."

"Nat, you're doing a *wonderful* job. Alex is on the straight and narrow for the time being. What the pair of you do in your spare time doesn't bother me. I'll only step in if it starts to affect how you do your job. I can't see it ever being a problem, though, and I couldn't be happier."

"Really?" I gasped, amazed. Was it really as easy as that? Could Alex and I be together? I needed to stop being so paranoid. Everyone who knew seemed happy about us.

"You just keep up the good work and everything will turn out fine." Gina smiled kindly as she reached for her bag. "Things may get complicated when the band gets back together, but I'm sure you'll be able to handle them. They're a lovely group of lads once you get to know them." I couldn't help but notice the humor in her eyes. "Isn't it crazy? I still think of them as boys even though they're men now."

"You were with them from the start, Gina. I'm sure it's easy to picture them that way. They were global icons, after all."

"Let's just hope that Matt and Alex talk soon, or there will be no reunion tour."

"Is the history between them really that bad?"

" I don't know all the ins and outs, but I do know that their friendship was ruined by a stupid mistake."

"A mistake?" I questioned with a frown. "Are you trying to tell me this was all over one falling out?"

"Alex and Matt were always bickering. One day they had a fight too many."

"Why didn't the other band members intervene?"

"You can't break up a fight between those two. Once you've seen them, you'll understand why." Now I knew what Shane meant about spending most of his time protecting the band from themselves rather than the fans.

"I'm not putting you off, am I?" I must have had a worried look on my face.

"No, I'm just concerned for Alex. He's so tense about this

meeting. Can't you speak to Matt and tell him to stop putting it off? It isn't getting them anywhere."

"I've already talked to him. He assured me that he'll turn up for the next meeting." That was only three days away. Hopefully Alex would be able to relax and finally focus on the tour after that.

"That's good. Alex will be pleased."

"He's lucky to have you looking out for him, Nat. It will be interesting to watch him try to hide his feelings for you from the band." I hadn't considered that but I knew she was right. Alex would want to keep our relationship secret from them, too, for the time being. How would we manage that while on tour? We'd all be working very closely together. "Don't look so scared. Alex cares a great deal for you. He'll protect you. It's what he does for the people he loves." Was she implying he'd done that before? Of course he had! Alex had a life before me! I wasn't so naive to think that I was the only woman he'd ever had feelings for.

A soft tap came at the door and I couldn't help the grin that spread across my face when Alex walked through.

"Are you ladies finished yet? I wanted to take Nat to dinner. She needs to get ready." I looked at my watch. Shit! Where had the time gone? I hadn't realized Gina and I had been chatting for that long.

"We're done, Alex. You two go and enjoy your meal."

"You better move your ass, Sexy. I don't want to be late to the restaurant." He smacked my butt as I rushed past him. I didn't even have time to peck his lips. I literally only had minutes to get ready!

"Do you want your hair up or down?" Diego asked, helping me into my tight black dress.

"Down. It's quicker!" I stressed, reaching for my makeup.

"Breathe. You can keep the rockstar waiting, you know. Keep him keen. Give him blue balls for once," Diego teased me with a nudge.

"I heard that!" Alex shouted from the other room. "Don't listen to a word he's saying, Nat!" The pleading tone in his voice made me giggle.

It didn't take Diego long to do my makeup. Alex was pacing back and forth at that point, waiting for me. Patience wasn't something he was very good at. I'd even thrown him a chocolate bar to pacify him, but it only kept him busy for a few minutes.

"There you go, Cupcake. Don't let Alex smudge your lipstick straight away. You don't look like the easy type." After swatting my butt, Diego pushed me towards Alex.

"Finally," he teased, circling his arms around me. "You look beautiful, Straight Lace." All I could do was smile in response as his lips pressed urgently against mine. Diego sighed behind me, but I didn't really care about my lipstick right then.

"We're going on your *bike*?" I gasped as he handed me a helmet. Alex's Harley was legendary, but Shane had once told me that he only rode it alone.

"Is that a problem? You're not scared, are you?"

"Are you kidding? I've wanted to go on this bike since I was a kid!" My excitement was obvious. Alex let out a loud laugh and shook his head.

"You're not that much younger than me, Nat. Don't make me sound so *old*." I got onto the bike behind him and hugged him tight. "Whoa. Don't hold me *too* tight. I need to breathe," he joked, looking at me over his shoulder. I was still beaming like a

Cheshire cat.

Alex's bike was fast. I loved the adrenaline rush that I got as we rode. The growl of the engine sent tremors through my body. With my arms around his waist, I held on tight as Alex accelerated. The sudden rush of wind made my hair that was free from the helmet dance frantically behind my back. The world around us was flashing by so fast it was a blur. I couldn't get enough of this feeling. I'd never felt so free on an open road before.

Alex took us to a secluded restaurant on the outskirts of LA. It was lit up with hundreds of twinkle lights and had ivy climbing the walls of the whitewash building.

"Where did you find this place?" I asked as he entwined his fingers with mine. "It's really pretty."

"I found it on my last ride up here. It looked like our kind of place." I knew he meant no one would interrupt us here, which I was really looking forward to. It wasn't very easy to find places outside of his mansion that we could be together.

He allowed me to go in first. The restaurant was empty. A single table laid up for two was all I could see. "You booked out the entire restaurant, didn't you?" Realisation hit me. His actions always took my breath away.

"I wanted to apologise for my outburst earlier. The way I treated you in front of my personal trainer was wrong of me."

"You should have brought him instead. He was the one you shouted at." Truthfully, his outburst had me more concerned than offended.

"I don't think of you as a possession. If you thought…"

"Alex, I know." Touching the side of his face, I tried to make him understand. "You didn't have to do all of this to prove it to me." I waved my arms around at his grand gesture.

"It's just…I've been so stressed these last few weeks. I don't want to mess *this* up. You mean too much to me. You know that, right?"

"You need to stop worrying about that. I'm not going anywhere. You couldn't get rid of me even if you paid me to leave. Like it or not, you're stuck with me." I nudged him playfully with my shoulder so he knew I was teasing.

I took a seat at the table, beckoning him with my eyes to join me. "Gina has spoken to Matt. He's not going to back out of the next meet up. She's told him he has no choice."

"She said that?"

"Yes. It's been eating away at you, and don't try to deny it. It's like Matt is torturing you before you've even met.

"He knows which buttons to press, that's for sure."

"You shouldn't let him get to you." Alex smirked at me as I spoke. "What?"

"You think it's that easy? Straight Lace, you wait until you meet him."

"Should I be worried?"

"Not when you're with me," he winked. I wasn't sure if he was joking or not. "I'm not suffocating you then?"

I looked over at him over my menu. "Why would you think that?"

"The life I lead isn't easy. I don't want my lifestyle to push you away."

"How many times do I have to tell you before you believe me? I'm in *love* with you, Alex Harbour. That's never going to change."

"Love doesn't always hold someone."

"Do you think you're the only one that's scared? I know what this world tour is going to mean. You're going to stir up the Steel Roses hysteria again. I was there the first time around, gazing up at you from down below. Now you're being thrust back into the limelight, and I'm worried you'll walk away from me. You're *Alex Harbour,* after all. You could have any woman you wanted in the entire *world.*"

"I could, but none of them would inspire me like you do." Stretching across the table, he took a strand of my hair between his fingers. "You're it for me, Straight Lace. I was hooked the moment I set eyes on you." My heart soared at the intensity of his gaze. "You must have known that deep down. All that pushing and pulling. It was our sexual desire for each other."

"That's not quite how I remember it. You were a real asshole to begin with." I giggled, taking his hand in mine over the table.

"That's because you kept denying me!"

"You were better once you lost the ego."

"You thought I had an ego?" He was playing along, pretending to look offended.

"You still do," I snorted, looking down at my menu. "But it's okay. I can live with it."

"Ouch. You wound me!"

"You'll get over it. Can we order? I'm starving." I grinned over at him and all he could do was chuckle.

"You can have whatever you want." I swallowed at the hidden meaning that was laced in his tone. Would he take me across this table right now? *That* was what I wanted. The hungry look in his eyes made me think he could read my mind. "You'll have to wait until later to have me. I'm not really in the mood for an audience." When he tilted his head towards the two waiters in the corner of the room, the puzzled look on my face dropped. I hadn't even noticed them.

"I have no idea what you mean. I want food," I smirked, licking my lips.

"Liar!" He winked playfully. "But you're right. Let's eat."

The food was delicious. I was at the point that if I ate anything else I would burst. Alex seemed a lot more relaxed considering he hadn't had a drop of alcohol. Sure, he'd slipped up a few times in the last month. He was a recovering addict, after all, and it was to be expected on occasion. Truthfully, I'd rather he slip with the drink than the drugs if there was a choice. Both were large demons for him to face, but the drugs had always seemed to take such a hold of him in the past. Luckily, the rehab center had been able to get him off the heroin. He'd been clean for almost eight months now.

"Thank you for a lovely evening," I yawned, falling into bed once we'd arrived back.

"You need to stop thanking me, Straight Lace. You're my girl. I want to spoil you." I tried to hide my inner squeal, but I loved it when he called me that. "You like me calling you my girl, huh?" Before I could blink, he'd pinned me to the mattress and gripped my wrists with his strong hands.

"Just a little." I gasped as his lips made a trail of kisses down my neck.

"I think it's more than a little." I could hear the smile in his voice as his hands began to move down my body. "You *are* my girl, though. When I'm out on stage again, all I'll see is you. I wouldn't even be considering this without you."

"That's not true. You're doing this for your fans, too. I

don't have to be the only reason, Alex. You don't need to put me on this pedestal." When he looked up, our eyes met and I was struck down with admiration and love.

"You can think what you like, but you *are* the reason any of this is happening. You brought me back to life. You've made me see the world again. I don't need to be consumed by drink and drugs because I have you." I didn't even realize that a single tear had escaped my eye until Alex wiped it away with his thumb. "Don't cry, Straight Lace. I was trying to be romantic," he teased, kissing my lips softly.

"I love you, Alex," I murmured against his lips, breathing him in deeply.

"I know you do," he sighed, kissing me deeper.

CHAPTER THREE

I was so apprehensive I couldn't stand still. Pacing my office, I watched the time tick by, praying that Alex's meeting with Matt and the band was going well. He'd been gone three hours already. I'd attempted to focus on work, but my mind kept wandering back to Alex. I had no idea how this meeting was going to affect him.

Shane suddenly appeared at the door. "Alex is back. He's gone straight to his room. He won't talk to anyone." My heart ached in my chest at those words. Why did he shut people out like this?

"I'll go and see if he'll talk to me."

It felt silly that I was nervous as I stood outside our bedroom door. I may have known Alex better than anyone, but he had so many layers to him. Honestly, I wasn't sure what I'd find behind that door and it terrified me.

There was no sign of him when I walked into the room. He must have been on the balcony. Cautiously, I made my way outside.

Alex was sitting with his back to me, shirtless, strumming his guitar. Playing this way always seemed to relax him, and I wasn't sure if interrupting was the best idea. Maybe he needed some time to clear his head.

"Don't go," he suddenly called, dropping his guitar as I began to back away. I stood frozen. How did he know I was there? Turning around, he gave me a small smile. "Stay with me." Without a word, I stepped towards him and sank down onto his lap. His arms encircled me and pulled me close against his chest.

"I'm here, Alex," I whispered, brushing my lips against his. He responded by capturing my head between both his hands and kissing me hard. Our lips never parted and we kissed so furiously that I wanted to climb inside his skin. I couldn't get close enough to him. My nails dug into his shoulders as his lips moved down my neck and towards the swell of my breasts. Through my dress, I rubbed my sex against the bulge in his pants. I knew what he needed to make sense of all the madness in his head. Undoing his button, I freed him quickly from the confines of his jeans as he began biting my neck. His hands moved lower and gripped my butt, squeezing and stroking as they went.

"I need you, Nat," he groaned into my chest.

"Take me then," I pleaded. "I'm yours."

Pulling my panties to the side, Alex was suddenly inside me. We began to move slowly against each other at first, allowing our bodies to enjoy the glorious sensations. He pulled my dress down, freeing my breasts, and when his mouth latched onto one of my nipples, I let out a cry of pleasure. I was already starting to build as Alex slammed me hard down on his cock.

"That's it, Baby. I need to hear you." That was never a problem and he knew it. I was *always* loud when we had sex. That's what he did to me. Tilting me back, he began to really fuck me. I let out a small cry of pleasure. At this angle he had full access to my breasts, which he began to bite and suck in turn.

Moments later, we almost came as one, my trembling orgasm setting off his. We clung to each other afterwards in a content silence.

"Matt's still a bitter fucker. He's willing to do this tour, but doesn't want anything to do with me behind the scenes. He's just in it for the money. He thinks I owe him and wants a higher percentage of the profits."

"He can't do that. You're the front man. The fans come to see *you*!" I don't know why I was so angry. Perhaps it was because I could feel what Matt had done to him. I could feel the tension in his body.

"Wow! I can see whose side you're on," he chuckled, running his hands through my hair. "It's very comforting."

"Good," I beamed, pecking his lips. "I've always got your back."

"And I've always got your ass," Alex teased, slapping my butt. "You stopped me from having a drink, Nat."

"I did?" I gasped at his confession, moving to look him in the eyes. It was then that I noticed the whiskey bottle on the table next to him.

"Every time I went to open it, I saw your face and the disappointment that I knew would be there. That's why I picked up my guitar instead."

"I'm so proud of you, Alex. But even if you had taken a sip, I'd never be disappointed in you."

"I don't want to ever let you down. I don't ever want you to look at me the way..." He stopped mid-sentence, his eyes full of pain.

"It's okay, you don't have to explain. You'll tell me when you're ready. I know you will."

"You have so much faith in me."

"Yes, I do," I grinned. "Now take me to our bed." Alex didn't need to be told twice.

"Do you think these shorts show too much?" Diego asked, spinning around.

"Well, I can see both butt cheeks. Is that the look you wanted?" I snorted.

"Bitch, I have a fabulous ass."

"I never said you didn't. You also have better legs than me. You should definitely get those shorts."

"You need to get that purple dress, too. It will be perfect for the charity event on Friday. Are you nervous?" It was the first public appearance for Steel Roses before they announced the world tour next month. The hype around the rumors was now in full force. Rock Records had planned this meeting to stir the press into a frenzy.

"More excited than anything. I'm nervous for Alex, though."

"Shane and I have taken bets as to who will throw the first punch. My bet is on Matt. You can never trust the lead guitarist."

"That's awful. You're meant to be their friends!"

"You don't know what they're like, Baby Cakes. Just wait and see. I really hope they don't bring out Alex's bad side this time around."

"He doesn't have a bad side," I joked, looking at a few clothes on the rail in front of me.

"You are blinded by love. He's not *that* perfect. I've

wondered if he has different sized balls. There has to be *something* wrong with that body of his." I put my hand over my mouth to stifle the loud laugh that threatened to escape. "I'll take that as a yes."

"Think whatever you want," I giggled. "Where's that dress I tried on earlier?" I asked, changing the subject. I loved my shopping trips with Diego. They were always eventful.

"It's over here. Maybe you should get the pink one, too."

"Why?"

"Baby Cakes, you can never have enough dresses." He still had a lot to teach me and he knew it.

The truth was that the content of my wardrobe had grown since moving to LA. My style had also changed. I hardly wore shorts and vest tops anymore. It was mostly little sundresses or skirts. Alex liked to have full access to my body at all times, and I had to admit, I enjoyed it, too.

My hair was often down these days, as well. It was amazing how someone's love could give you so much confidence. Not that he had confessed his love for me yet, but I could see it in his eyes every time he touched me. Love had never been easy for Alex—that was obvious—and I wasn't going to put any pressure on him. He'd tell me when he was ready.

"Did you buy the entire store again?" Alex teased, watching me set my bags on the floor.

"You know what Diego is like. He even tried to get me into the hairdressers to change my hair colour."

"You don't need to change that. You're perfect as you are."

"You're very sweet today," I giggled. "Have you eaten yet?"

"No, I was waiting for you. By the way, Gina told me that the schedule for the tour rehearsals has been finalized. She'll send it over in the morning."

"Oh, really?" Alex nodded. "How are you feeling about that?" I asked, joining him on the bed.

"I'm looking forward to seeing if the magic is still there. We weren't the closest band friendship wise, but we always came together when it was about the music."

"I still can't believe I'm going to see you all on the same stage!"

"Careful, Straight Lace, your groupie side is showing again."

"I don't care," I laughed. "Do you think you'll write some new material with them?" I tried not to show my enthusiasm at the idea, but the thought of Alex writing Steel Roses music again made me a little giddy.

"I'm not sure. You need trust to collaborate, and Matt and I don't have that anymore."

"Maybe in time you will," I said hopefully, running my hands down his chest.

"Yeah, maybe." He smiled shyly. It wasn't an Alex-type smile. "I could end up writing songs with Matt about you."

"I thought you didn't want the band to know about us?" Surely if he started writing love songs with Matt, it would start all kinds of rumors.

"To start with, yes—I don't want you to be pulled into anything—but when the time is right, I want the whole world to know." *The world?* Swallowing hard, I widened my eyes at him.

"Don't look so frightened. It's all about timing. Your protection is my main priority." Smiling softly, he leaned in to peck my lips. "You might run for the hills before I get that chance, though."

"Why do you say that? You know how I feel about you."

"This is the calm before the storm, Nat. Feelings can change."

This had something to do with the band, and before I could stop myself the words fell out of my mouth. "Are you going to tell me what happened before we go on tour?"

Alex sighed deeply, pinching the bridge of his nose. "I'll have to. Matt will do it for me if not." I still didn't really understand why he was keeping it from me. "I want to tell you, Nat. I really do. I'm just afraid you'll see me differently once you know the truth. You must remember that in the early Steel Roses days, I was a different person. I was consumed with fame and fortune. It was all I saw for such a long time."

"I don't know why you're so worried about telling me. I love you. The good and bad. I know about your demons, and it only makes me love you more."

"She was called Vanessa." His voice was so quiet I hardly heard the name. Was he telling me *right now?*!

"Who was?" My mouth was suddenly very dry. I was asking a question I already knew the answer to.

"The woman we both loved." I swallowed hard. Their fight was all over a woman. Not just any woman, either. I remembered the awful news clippings about Vanessa. From what I'd read, I knew she had been Matt's long term girlfriend. Alex touched the cross on his chest. That one small gesture told me that the tattoo there was in honor of *her*. Suddenly I had a sinking feeling. Did I really want to hear this? "Ness was there right at the start. We all met at college. She had a thing for younger guys. Matt and I were only two of her many admirers."

"Alex, I'm not sure I…"

"I need to get this all out right now. I'm not sure I'll ever have the strength to do it again. Please, Nat," he begged, touching my hand that had moved onto his chest. I nodded, snuggling deeper into his arms. I wasn't sure I could look him in the eye while he told me. "When Steel Roses began doing the Campus tours, Ness began attending every show. I was already getting a lot of attention from the females and I fucking loved it. Ness caught Matt's attention first, and they were dating by the time we got our first record deal." His hands were rhythmically stroking my hair. "She was a real flirt—that was just her nature —but something inside me changed when I was around her. Her smell, the way she walked, how her lips curled into a smile. I slowly became obsessed with the one woman that I couldn't have. It began to eat away at me, and I got lost on the drink and drugs. It was the only way I could shut her out." I stopped breathing at his confession. His demons had started because of a *woman.* "Milly could see what was going on and called Ness out on it one evening while we were all out. What I didn't expect was for Ness to admit that she had feelings for me, too."

"The two of you had an affair behind Matt's back?" I gasped, horrified. Now I was beginning to understand where this deep rooted hatred had stemmed from.

"We tried to fight it, believe me, but we loved each other."

"So you and Matt were writing songs about the same woman and he had no idea?" I couldn't look up at him.

"We kept our affair a secret for years. Steel Roses was gaining popularity. Gina wouldn't allow our secret to come out and destroy the band. It tore me in two watching Matt and Ness together. She was meant to be mine. I was the one she wanted to be with. We tried to break it off so many times over the years, but we always ended up back together. We were like magnets. The force was unexplainable." His hands moved from my hair. "Look at me, Nat. I need to see your face." I was immobile. Truthfully, I didn't *want* to move. "Whatever I felt for her is nothing compared to how I feel about you. You *have* to understand that." Hesitantly, I looked up and gave him a small smile even while feeling insignificant. "She was everything that was bad for me. *You* are all that's good. You must see that."

"Alex, I know what happened to her." My voice was so quiet I didn't think he heard me. I needed to hear the truth, though, so I spoke a little louder. "I remember the press release. Tell me you had nothing to do with it."

"Gina told us that we could never go public with our affair. We had too much to lose. Ness went off the rails, ranting that if she couldn't be with me, she didn't want to live. I never thought she'd O.D. Milly found her body the next day when Ness wouldn't answer her calls. After what had happened with Gina, I thought she just needed time. I was wrong. Matt was in bits over it, and it took everything I had to try to keep myself together. I'd lost the only woman I loved up to that point. What I didn't know was that Ness had left Matt a note at their home in London, telling him everything." I'd never seen him cry before, but he had tears trickling down his face as he spoke. Wanting to comfort him, I reached out and hugged him tightly. "I'll never forget seeing his face in the record studio, or the hatred burning in his eyes. He only muttered two words to me before hitting me and leaving. '*Why her?*' Those words have been haunting me ever since. If I hadn't pursued Ness in the first place, she'd still be alive. She was my best friend's woman and I had an affair with her for almost six years."

"This is what's been eating away at you for so long? Why did you allow the press to paint you as a monster?"

"I needed to be punished somehow. I was getting all this success with my solo career and it felt all wrong. Matt was fading into darkness and I had everything."

"How could you think that? People fall in love with the wrong people all the time. Look at me with David!"

"You *weren't* in love with him, trust me. You've only ever had eyes for me." A small smirk played on his face.

"You know what I mean. Alex, you can't blame yourself. Ness was an adult and made her own choices. Besides, it was wrong of Gina to make you hide your feelings from Matt. It would have been difficult, but in time he would have moved on. That's life."

"Ness was poison for me, Nat. Gina and Milly could see that. I let the pain of not being able to have Ness swallow me up, and I drowned in it. She knew it bothered me that she was with Matt when she was alive, and she used to rub it in my face if we were on a break. She'd be all over him just to make me jealous. That was when I started injecting heroin. She was goading me to do it. I could see it in her eyes. It did more than just get me high, though. It numbed the pain, and when I realized that, I became dependent on it."

"This tattoo is in memory of her, isn't it?" I ran my fingertips over the outline of the cross with wings on his chest. He stopped my hand by gripping it with his.

"I owed it to her, Nat. I had to honor her somehow. It was all my fault." His beautiful face looked lifeless.

Taking a deep breath, I gazed deeply into his eyes. "It's okay. We both had a past before we found each other. I understand. It doesn't make me love you any less." Deep in my heart I knew that was true.

"It doesn't?" Alex didn't look like he believed me. "I'm not a good man, Nat, but for you I want to try. I want to be someone you deserve."

"You *are* a good man. You just don't believe in yourself. Matt has a right to be in pain, but he needs to remember that Ness was as much to blame as you were. He can't try to punish you for the rest of your life. You both have to lay it to rest at some point."

"He's not willing to do that. He's going to make this tour as difficult as possible. I know how his mind works. He'll be underhanded and cunning. He's such a selfish son of a bitch these days."

"You can rise above anything. You're Alex Harbour, the front man of Steel Roses," I teased, nudging him gently.

"With you by my side, I think you might be right." He spoke so sincerely.

"Well, I'm not going anywhere." Running his hands through his hair, Alex let out a sigh of relief. "Are you glad you've finally told me?"

"I don't know why I waited so long in the first place," he admitted.

"It's not easy reliving a painful past, but I'm glad you've finally come clean so I can support you."

"What did I ever do to deserve you?" he muttered, cupping my face with his hand. "Fuck, do you have any idea what you mean to me?" I giggled as his lips crashed against mine. I did know, but I couldn't wait for him to say the actual words.

CHAPTER FOUR

The moment I stepped out of the limo I realized that my heels were too high. Damn Diego for making me wear them. I was going to look like a newborn giraffe walking down the red carpet.

"You okay?" Alex frowned, noticing my discomfort.

"It's these stupid shoes," I pouted. "I told Diego I didn't want to wear them." Alex shook his head, smiling at me. "If I fall, will you help me up?"

"You won't fall, Straight Lace. I've got you." Putting his arm through mine, he pulled me closer to his side. "It gives me a reason to keep you close tonight anyway." I smiled nervously as excited screams came from behind us. Matt Higgins was making his way up the red carpet with a tall, elegant blonde woman that I recognized from somewhere. "Here goes nothing," Alex whispered nervously, squeezing my waist.

I watched Matt's jaw tightened when he spotted us. The pain and hatred was deep in his brown eyes. Even after all the time that had passed, he was still a good looking guy. His long, messy, dirty blonde hair hadn't changed since the Steel Roses days, but his face was more distinguished than before. He was a lot leaner than Alex; his tux fit well tonight. His tired, worn eyes made me wonder if he was still a drug user, though.

"Good evening, Matthew." Alex spoke first, and as he did, I could feel his body go rigid with tension. "I didn't expect you to bring Lola." The blonde looked at him in disgust. "How have you both been?"

"My sister is no longer your concern," Matt spat. "Are you deliberately trying to be an asshole?"

"I was just making conversation," Alex pointed out. "I'd like to introduce Natasha..."

"Like fuck you were, and I don't want to meet another one of your tarts! I want nothing to do with either of you!" With that, Matt stormed off down the red carpet. Wow, and I thought Alex was an asshole the first time I met him. Matt was far worse.

"I'm sorry about that," Alex winced, looking down at me. "He just assumes..."

"It's fine. I've been called far worse," I winked.

"That didn't actually go as bad as I imagined," he chuckled. "He wasn't violent this time, at least." Turning, my eyes widened at the sight of Cody Donovan and Mason Maxwell making their way down the red carpet after us. "Breathe, Straight Lace. It's only every member of Steel Roses in one place for the first time in ten years." The bastard! He knew what a big deal this was to me!

"Thanks, that really helps." I rolled my eyes at him while my inner school girl was silently hyperventilating. How long had I waited for this moment? These guys were *legends*. Cody —the bass player—had always been the quirky member of the band. Tonight he was wearing a purple suede suit, which was his typical attire. His long dark hair was now streaked with grey, but it suited him. Mason was the meathead of the band, and the drummer. His arms were pure muscle, but the beats he'd played over the years needed that. He'd always had a shaved head, too. When I thought about it, Alex was the only one that had really changed from the early Steel Roses days. His solo fame had molded him into the rock star he was today.

"You're looking very dapper, Mr. Harbour," Mason teased, nudging Alex with his shoulder. "I'm surprised you left your leather at home though. Who is this lovely lady?" Swallowing hard, I forced a smile. It wasn't easy being surrounded by my childhood idols, even if I was dating one of them now.

"This is my PA, Nat."

"Your PA, you say?" Cody beamed. "So we'll be seeing a lot more of you, Nat. Are you sure you're ready to work with all of us? Milly was a little unsure at first."

"I've always enjoyed a challenge. If I can handle working with Alex, I'm sure I'll cope with the rest of you." I looked up at Alex, who was gazing down at me with admiration.

"Nat can handle me better than Milly, if I'm being honest." I was taken aback at his comment.

"Whoa, you must be quite a find then!" Cody patted Alex on the back. "How'd it go with Matt?"

"Icy. You could have told me that he was bringing Lola."

"Lola is here, too? What was he *thinking*?" Mason looked shocked.

"He doesn't think," Cody snapped, glaring ahead. "That's his fucking problem."

"Let's just find our seats. Perhaps he'll chill out after a few drinks?" Alex and Cody didn't look very confident at Mason's statement. I was glad Shane and a few of his guys were nearby. I really hoped the night didn't end in a fist fight but I wasn't going to hold my breath.

The charity gala was full of LA's rich and famous. You'd think that I'd be used to these events by now, but it was much easier being behind the scenes. When I attended as Alex's *kind of* date, I actually had to have conversations with these people.

I sat opposite two supermodels that were drooling over Alex, and an annoying teenage popstar that really should have had a chaperone.

"Is he old enough to drink?" I joked in Alex's ear.

"Who, Mikey Stardust? He does look about ten, doesn't he? Do you think we should order him some milk?" I giggled, moving my attention to a table a few feet away. Lola was with Matt and couldn't keep her eyes off Alex.

"What's the deal with Lola?" I asked, a little curious. "She's been staring at you all night." Alex took a sip of water before draping his arm over the back of my chair and moving closer to me.

"She's always had a bit of a crush on me."

"Really? Who hasn't?" I snorted, raising my eyebrow at him. "You've fucked her, haven't you? How long ago?" I could read his eyes so well.

"It was years ago, not long after the band split up."

"Shit, was she even legal then?" I was joking, but she did look a little young.

"Of course she was. She's older than you. In all honesty, I don't remember sleeping with her. With all the women over the years, their faces started blurring together. Your face is the only one that stayed in focus long after you left. That's how I knew you were different."

"Judging by the way her tongue hangs out when she looks at you, I'd say Lola still has a crush."

"Are you even listening to what I'm saying? Stop eyeballing her." I wasn't even aware I was doing that.

"Sorry, I was listening."

"Your possessive side turns me on, Straight Lace. Be careful or this entire gala will know that you're my girl once I lay you over this table."

"You wouldn't dare." I felt his hand on my leg under the table, massaging my thigh before drifting higher.

"Try me." Alex had a playful look in his eye and I knew he was serious. I'd have to back down and quick. I wasn't ready for the whole world to know about us yet.

"Would you like some more water?" I smiled sweetly, pushing his hand away and then reaching for the bottled water on the table.

"Yes, please." He smirked before joining in on the conversation with the couple sitting next to him.

The press swarmed Alex once we left the gala. They were all shouting at the same time, asking about the possible Steel Roses reunion tour and whether he and Matt had made up. They must have noticed the frosty confrontation earlier.

The other band members were still partying inside. A recovering alcoholic, Alex wasn't quite the party animal these days. He coped better when he took himself out of temptation's way and I was proud of him for it. He really wanted to face his demons this time.

"You did well tonight," Shane commented as he opened the limo door for Alex and me. "I really thought I'd be breaking up fights."

"There will be plenty of time for that on the tour," Alex joked, pulling me onto his lap and kissing me hard. "Thank you for tonight."

"What did I do?" I asked, surprised at his sudden advance. He ran his thumb over my bottom lip, lost in thought.

"You kept me calm. That was so much easier than I thought it would be. Maybe the tour won't be so bad."

"Is it better now that I know everything?"

"Yes, Matt will paint me as the villain any chance he gets, but it won't bother me. You know me, Straight Lace, better than anyone."

"And you know me. I've grown so much with you. I don't feel like a wallflower anymore. You've brought me out of myself."

"I saw the beauty in you the moment we met. I'm good at reading people."

"Oh, really?" I giggled. "You only wanted one thing from me when we first met."

"I did, but I quickly realized that I needed more."

"You were still an arse, though." Alex let out a loud chuckle. "But you're *my* arse."

"That I am." He grinned, capturing my lips with his.

The hysteria among the press only worsened after the charity gala. Everyone was talking about the possible Steel Roses reunion. Some claimed it would be a one off show, while others were closer to the truth with talks of a world tour. Alex's social media was a lot harder to control, that was for sure.

"Have you got a spare moment, Nat?" Gina asked, appearing at my door.

"Of course. I'm trying to sort out Alex's social media. I could do with a break." Gina took a seat in front of me. She looked a little perplexed, which wasn't like her.

"This isn't easy to say, Nat." My eyes snapped up. "Rock Records is forbidding you to have a relationship with Alex."

"Excuse me?" I choked. "What right do they…?"

"I'm coming to you first because I know Alex is going to fly off the handle when he finds out. They're worried about the effect it might have on the tour if the fans discover Alex is in a relationship. Honestly, I have no idea how they found out about the pair of you in the first place, but they know."

"Do you realize how ridiculous this is?"

"It's been written into the contract, Nat. Alex must be seen to his fans as a single man throughout the course of the tour."

"The tour is for an entire year!" I fumed. "Are you telling me I've got to watch groupie after groupie go to these after show parties and throw themselves at Alex for a full year! That is bullshit! He won't stand for it!"

"I know, that's why I'm coming to you first. You were planning on keeping your relationship a secret anyway, right? *That* is your way around this. Alex will look for any excuse to break from his contract, so you have to make him see sense and sign. It's just one year and then the two of you can do whatever you want."

"Gina, he's going to go fucking crazy no matter how I try to handle this."

"They wanted me to fire you." What the hell? They couldn't do that! "I've calmed the situation by telling Rock Records that it's just a casual fling—that it won't interfere with the tour." My mind was racing. Alex wasn't going to take this well, but Gina was right. He had to sign the contract. What was a year, anyway? Alex and I would have the rest of our lives together once it was over. We'd kept our relationship a secret for this long; we could do it for a little longer.

"I'll talk to him."

"We need to do it together. I need to know you're on my side. The tour *must* come first. Are we both agreed?" I nodded, feeling my heart drop in my chest. I may not have liked the situation, but I knew Gina was right. This was for Alex, after all.

It took a while to find where he was hiding. We eventually found him in the music room, softly strumming his guitar, and eating his favorite chocolate . My stomach twisted uncomfortably at the thought of what I was about to do. This conversation wasn't going to be easy.

"Has someone died?" he asked, looking at our concerned faces. Gina turned to me, urging me to start.

"Alex, we need to talk about something, but you need to promise me that you won't fly off the handle."

"That depends on what you're going to say, Nat. Honestly, I don't like the tone in your voice."

"Nothing is going to change between us. I need you to remember that." Alex looked at me puzzled, then moved his eyes to Gina for an explanation.

"Rock Records has found out about your relationship."

"WHAT!?" He was up out of his chair in an instant. "How the *fuck* did they find out?!"

"I don't know, Alex. It was just as much of a shock to me. You and Nat have been so careful."

"What have those fuckers said? Wait, let me guess—they're giving me a girlfriend ban again?" *Again?*

Gina nodded. "It's been written into your contract for the world tour."

"The entire fucking tour? You have *got* to be joking!" He started pacing back and forth, pulling at his hair. "I won't fucking sign then. They can't do this. It's my fucking *life* they're playing with! Nat means too much to me, Gina. I will *not* give her up...*ever*! I'll fucking fight this!"

"You don't have to." When I moved towards him, he opened his arms and pulled me into an embrace. "We weren't planning to go public for a while anyway. What difference does a year make? Do you really want a media circus before the tour even starts? I know you can fight this and get the best lawyers, but what's the point in going through all that if we were planning to hide our relationship for a while anyway?"

"You're on board with this?" Pulling back to look at me, his eyes searched mine. "It's the *entire* tour, Nat. I have to act single any time I'm in public. That won't *bother* you?" I tried to hide the fear in my eyes while nodding, but he could see straight through me. "You're not okay with this."

"Alex, you have no choice," Gina interrupted. "If you walk away now, you'll be walking away from the opportunity of a lifetime. Look at the hype you've stirred already! Don't be stupid."

"You really think I give a fuck about any of that? If it came down to the tour or Nat, she'd win every fucking time. Don't assume you have any hold on my life, Gina, because you don't! Doing this tour is *my* choice! I could walk right now and never think twice!"

"Stop this, Alex. We can still be together, we'll just need to be careful. You can't throw all of this away. I won't let you. Nothing is going to change, I promise." Alex already had too much to deal with. I didn't want our relationship to add to his problems.

"You can't promise that, Nat." His clear blue eyes looked so lost. I wanted to jump inside and pull him back into the light.

"Can you leave us please, Gina?" I muttered. She nodded slightly, then silently walked out of the room. "Promise me you won't use this as an excuse to pull out of the tour."

"What?" Alex gasped, letting me go. My words had wounded him.

"You heard me." I knew I needed to be firm with him. It was the only way. "I know you can fight this and win, but what good would that do? Our relationship is a secret, anyway. We both agreed that would be for the best. You're blowing this all out of proportion."

"Oh, am I?" Alex had a bemused grin on his face. "Are you having a go at me, Straight Lace?"

"You're being an argumentative asshole!" I exclaimed, shoving his chest and pulling away from him.

"I'm not. I'm putting you first."

"As much as I appreciate the gesture, you don't have to do that."

"Rock Records always does this. A girlfriend ban at my age is ridiculous!"

"If it keeps your fans happy it's worth it. It doesn't bother me, honestly. I'm always going to be right here."

"How did I win you? I'm in love with you, Straight Lace, you know that, right?" My heart leapt at his words, and before I knew it I was back in his arms, his lips fiercely against mine.

"You love me," I panted against his mouth, feeling his body pin me against the wall.

"So fucking much. When you're not with me, I go fucking

crazy. You're deep inside my mind. You're all I think about. You won't let go and I never fucking want you to. You're mine, Straight Lace, do you understand that? You. Are. Fucking. Mine!" Something primal and animalistic ignited inside us. We started pulling at each other's clothes, not stopping until there was a pile on the floor.

Alex's hand gripped my legs, thrusting his growing erection against my sex. I threw my head back against the wall and dug my nails into his shoulder. His lips began to travel down my neck, biting and sucking as he went. Shivers of pleasure pulsed through my body.

"You taste so fucking sweet," he hummed in appreciation. "I'm going to fuck you against the wall, Straight Lace, so you'll never forget that this pussy is mine. Do you understand me?"

"Ugh, yes," I moaned, feeling his fingers slip inside my panties. He began to make slow circles while biting down gently on my neck. My senses went into overdrive, and I wrapped my legs tighter around him, pulling him as close as humanly possible.

"Do you want me inside you?" he purred before sucking on my earlobe. It was a bloody stupid question.

"Yes," I groaned, biting my lip. "Fuck me, Alex!"

"Tomorrow when you wake up you'll know this is mine." He cupped my sex, putting pressure on my clit to emphasize his words. With a primal growl, he pulled my panties to the side and quickly entered me. I could never get enough of feeling him fill me. He was aggressive as he fucked me up against the wall. I moaned wantonly each time he slammed into me, knowing it would never be enough. As his fingers dug into my butt cheeks, I wrapped my arms around his neck and allowed him to take me any way he wanted. I loved being claimed this way. It truly felt like I was his in moments like this.

It didn't take long for me to climax, and Alex followed soon after. When we were finished, we both stood breathless against the wall, still clinging onto each other.

Sedated and completely relaxed in his embrace, there was only one thing going through my mind. *Alex Harbour* had just told me he was in *love* with me.

I almost couldn't believe it. How did I get here?

CHAPTER FIVE

The opening in the curtains allowed the last of the evening sun to stream through the bedroom window.

"We've spent the entire afternoon in bed," I yawned, stretching over to run my hands down Alex's chest.

"And your point is?" He chuckled, moving to plant a kiss on my stomach. "I'd spend the whole *week* in bed with you if I could."

"It's a shame you have that meeting at Rock Records tomorrow." Alex groaned at the thought. "You better sign that damn contract, though. If you get back and I..."

"Baby, relax. You've given me more than a good talking to. We'll make it work. I'll be signing the contract so you don't need to worry."

"Will all the band be there?"

"No, we won't all be together again until the press conference next month. I think Gina is worried about us all kicking off if we meet sooner."

"You mean Matt kicking off?" Alex smiled softly, pulling me back into his arms. The feel of his bare skin against mine had such an effect on me. I melted into him.

"Matt is his own worst enemy and he doesn't have you fighting in his corner. Cody and Mason will diffuse some of the tension, though. Do you remember some of the outfits Cody used to wear back in the day?" I nodded with a grin. "The one thing we all always agreed on was that most of the time he looked like a total cock. His sense of style hasn't changed since those days, so I know we won't be arguing *all* the time."

"You all had your bad dress sense eras," I snorted, looking up at Alex. I couldn't help but giggle when he glared at me.

"I've always looked good! You can blame Diego if not!"

"The tie dye months didn't look good on you in the nineties."

"That shit was popular back then."

"You weren't some new age hippy, Alex. It was hilarious. You even mixed it with leather pants at one event. I remember the photos." I was laughing so hard that I had to sit up to catch my breath.

"I made it look good. Admit it!" He pulled me back down, pinning me against the mattress. "I could find some of that tie dye shit now and fuck you in it if you want."

"God, no!" I giggled. Alex began to nibble down my neck, his hands gravitating to the curve of my butt.

"What am I going to do with you? It's not nice to make fun of me." He growled into the crook of my neck.

"I think a good, hard fuck will sort me out."

"You think so?"

Nodding seductively, I pulled his face up to meet mine, and within moments we were lost in each other again.

"Are you getting enough time off? I don't like to think you're being taken advantage of." Rolling my eyes, I shook my head. My mother loved to worry. Why did I Skype her today? I should have just sent her a text message. "How are you and Alex?"

"Everything is fine, Mum. You don't need to worry."

"My baby is half way across the world. Of course I worry. Why haven't the two of you gone public yet? It's been almost four months! Doesn't Alex want to show you off?"

"He's protecting me. I'm the one who doesn't want to go public yet! Do you have any idea what it's going to be like for me when the press finds out about us? We'll be followed *everywhere*."

"Are you really sure about all this, Natty? Liv said you sounded distant on the phone last week. You haven't Skyped in ages, either. It's only been phone calls lately."

"Things are a bit hectic here at the moment." Looking up from my seat in the coffee house, I noticed Diego rushing in with panic on his face. It had only been half an hour since I had left Alex with the directors at Rock Records. I'd walked to the coffee shop next door so I could call my mum. What could possibly be going on now? All he had to do was sign the contract! "Mum, I've got to go. I'm needed." I hung up before she could answer just as Diego reached my table.

"You need to get back upstairs. It's all kicked off!" Diego was talking so fast that I hardly understood him.

"What do you mean? It's just Alex signing contracts, right?"

"There's a new boss at Rock Records. Alex knows him and all hell has broken loose. If you don't calm him down, I'm worried he'll be arrested."

Without waiting for him to finish, I took off running so fast I could feel my heart beating in time with my steps. I was in the lobby before I knew it, and then tapping my foot as I watched the lift slowly climb to the right floor.

When the doors pinged open, the first face I saw was Gina's. Right after that, I saw Shane holding Alex back.

"What the hell is going on?" I asked, my eyes instantly focusing on Alex.

"Ask the fucker in the boardroom!" he spat. "It all makes fucking sense now!" Looking at him puzzled, I urged him for more information. I had no idea what he was talking about.

"Natasha White! Well, isn't it a small world?" I froze at the voice coming from behind me. This had to be a sick joke. He couldn't be here! I turned slowly, only to be faced with the deep brown eyes I'd known and craved before Alex walked into my life.

"David?" I gasped. "W...What are you doing here?"

"You didn't hear the good news? I've been brought on as a Director at Rock Records. I'll be heading up publicity and live events."

"*What?*" I began to understand how Rock Records had found out about Alex and me. "Can I have a private chat with you for a moment, David?" I was starting to see red and didn't want anyone to watch me explode.

"I'm not leaving you alone in a room with this asshole!" Alex fumed. I cautioned him with my eyes. We were in a public place, so he needed to be careful. To the outside world, I was just his personal assistant.

"We can talk in my office. It will be just like old times." David said with a wink. I didn't turn around to look at Alex, but I heard a commotion and then Shane trying to reassure him that I knew what I was doing.

"You're looking good, Nat. LA is clearly treating you well." David smiled warmly, closing the door as I walked in to take a seat in front of his desk.

"Cut the bullshit, David! What the fuck are you doing taking a job at Rock Records?"

"It was a good career move for me."

"You would have been Vice President at Flavour Records in a few years! How is this a *good* career move?"

"I want to keep you safe." His eyes softened as he made his way across the room to me.

"Keep me *safe*? From *what*?"

"That loser rock star you think you're in love with. It's just a silly infatuation, Nat. It won't last. He'll break your heart someday soon, and when he does, I'll be here to catch you."

"What did you say to Alex to make him fly off the handle like that?"

"I said much the same to him. You're both fools if you think you have a future."

"You don't know what you're talking about! We love each other. You had your chance with me for over five years, David! You have no fucking right taking this job and doing this! You're the one who put that stupid girlfriend ban in Alex's contract, aren't you?"

"I'm not prepared to watch you being harassed by the media circus across the world, Nat. I care about you too much. I'm doing all of this to protect you."

"Oh, please. You're doing all this because you have a bigger ego than Alex! What? Are you pissed off because he won? Alex is *everything* to me! If you think you can break us up, you're wrong."

"You really think you'll be able to handle him being on tour with Steel Roses? Do you honestly think he'll be able to stay faithful when every one of his fans are falling all over him?"

"I have to believe that he will because he loves me."

David snorted loudly. "Is that what he told you? Nat, I thought you were smarter than this. You're like a deer trapped in the headlights. This isn't going to end well for you and it won't be long before you realize that. Get out while you can." He leaned down and looked at me in a way that I once craved. "You know I want you. I've *always* wanted you. I can give you more than he can." David was too close and my body began to shudder. When his finger traced my collarbone, I was up out of the chair in a heartbeat.

"Don't fucking touch me, David. If Alex..."

"You still want me, Nat. Admit it." He was delusional. The mere thought of him made my skin crawl.

"You're wrong. I don't want you anywhere near me."

"That's going to be difficult since I'm heading up the promo for the Steel Roses reunion. We're going to be working *very* closely together. It will be just like old times." He had a smug grin on his face, and by that time I'd heard enough.

"You're a fucking asshole!" I seethed, shoving past him.

"I'm looking forward to working with you again too, Nat," he called after me as I left his office.

Alex was waiting for me a few paces down the hall. Worry was etched all over his face.

"Are you okay?" I could tell he wanted to pull me into his arms, but there were too many people around.

"Just shocked."

Alex took my hand in his. "You're trembling? Did he..."

"I'm fine, Alex. I...I just need to get back to the house. I'll meet you there later, okay?" Pulling away from his hold wasn't easy but we were drawing too much attention, and at that moment, all I wanted was to be alone to collect my thoughts.

"Alex is upset, Baby Cakes." Diego always managed to find my hiding places in this house. Luckily, I'd had at least an hour to clear my head.

"What do you mean?"

"You running out on him like that."

"It wasn't like that! I just needed to be alone so I could think. It's not easy to get any time to yourself in this place. Why does he have to overreact all the time?"

"That's Alex. You know what he's like better than anyone." Diego ran his hands through his hair nervously. It looked like he was trying to work out how to say something. "You don't still have feelings for David, do you?"

"No! Why are you even asking?!" I was becoming more irate by the moment! Why couldn't I just be left alone for a few hours?

"It was just a question. No need to jump down my throat! I've always looked out for Alex. I just needed to be sure."

"Diego! I just want to be alone. Alex is a big boy. He'll be okay for a few hours. My old boss that I had an affair with is now heading the Steel Roses world tour. Do you have any idea how difficult this is for me?"

"You're not going to leave, are you? Alex won't..."

"I'm not going anywhere. I love Alex. Handling David is another matter, though. He likes to play dirty. I've watched him do it before."

"Are you saying he could make your life difficult?" I nodded sadly, looking down at the floor.

I knew David better than anyone. He had never been a good loser. To him, it had always been about the chase. That was what had made our affair so exciting, but I didn't want to be part of it anymore. David was in my *past.* Being with him was nothing like how I felt when Alex touched me. I'd thought I loved David at one point, but compared to the way I felt with Alex, I knew now that it had only been lust and infatuation. I wanted him back then because he belonged to someone else. Our tryst had been exciting and passionate, but it hadn't been deep rooted like the feelings I had for Alex. I'd never had a man take me over so completely. With my rock star, it was as if my life didn't matter, because if I didn't have him, I had nothing. That was a scary concept to wrap my mind around. I was in so deep with Alex that it frightened me. What if one day I wasn't enough for him? I couldn't go back to my old life in London even if I wanted to.

Why was I even thinking like this? Alex had confessed his love for me. He wasn't going anywhere. Would love be enough to keep us strong, though? It had to be. There was no other direction to go. All my roads led to Alex.

Besides, what could David really do to us? He may have been one of the directors at Rock Records, but Steel Roses was bigger than their record label. The label couldn't have *that* much control over them.

I had no idea how long I sat in the small seated area behind the pool house, but I was snapped from my thoughts by the sound of an aggressive voice.

"Put the fucking bottle down, Alex!" I knew it was Shane.

His voice was disapproving, and I had one guess as to what kind of bottle it was.

By the sound of it, Alex and Shane were arguing by the pool. It didn't take me long to walk from behind the building. My eyes instantly met with Alex.

"This is your way of coping?" I glared, looking down at the whiskey bottle in his hand.

"Where the fuck have you been? I thought you'd left!" I sighed in relief that he wasn't slurring. He couldn't have had too much—if any—to drink yet. Alex was so afraid that I would leave him. I often wondered if his mother dying when he was a child was part of the issue. Rock Records played on his sad childhood in the early days to make fans connect with him. It was something that Alex had never spoken to me about. He never mentioned either of his parents.

"I was behind the pool house. I just needed a bit of time. Give Shane the bottle, Alex. You don't need it."

"Don't I?" I hated it when his eyes looked so lost. "It's the one thing that never lets me down."

"You know that's not true."

"You left, Nat. You didn't even tell me what that fucker said to you."

"Have you never heard of needing a bit of space?" I sighed, moving to stand in front of him. My strong, fearless rock star looked so weak in that moment. While softly brushing his knuckles, I pulled the whiskey bottle out of his grasp and handed it to Shane. Once he had it, he promptly left Alex and me alone. "You really thought I'd left?" I questioned, running my hands down his chest. His breaths seemed to come in gasps, but he began to relax at my simple touch.

"I didn't know what he said to you, Straight Lace. You were fucking *shaking* when you walked out of his office!"

"It was the shock of seeing him again. I wasn't expecting it."

"How do you think I felt when he walked in *after* I'd signed the fucking contract?" Alex laughed in disbelief. "It was like some fucked up joke. If I'd known it was *that* fucker who had decided on the ban, I'd have taken him to court and spent my last dollar if I had to!"

"That's what he wants. David is looking for a reaction."

"I'll give him a fucking reaction!"

"I'm not saying it was an easy situation for you, but you do know why he did this, don't you?"

"To get back at us." My eyes widened. Alex already understood. "He told me that we wouldn't last, that I couldn't possibly hold on to you. He said that he was more worthy of you than I would ever be. I saw red. No one can love you like me, Nat. I don't care what he fucking says!"

"I know. You don't have to explain." Touching the side of his face, I ran my fingertips across his lips, which parted at my simple touch. "I don't want David. I want you, Alex. Never forget that."

"What if he's right, Straight Lace? What if I *am* all wrong for you? What if I ruin you like I've done to all the women that have loved me?"

"That's a risk I'm willing to take. I always knew this wasn't going to be easy. You're *Alex freaking Harbour*, after all. Chaos has a habit of following you around."

Alex finally chuckled, pulling me into his warm embrace. "It seems to follow you around, too. Do you have any other crazy, stalker exes that I need to know about?"

"None that have enough qualifications to work for Rock Records."

"So you *do* have other crazy stalker exes?" I could feel his smirk as I buried my head in his chest. "Give me their names and I can beat their asses before they find out we're together."

"I'm not sure I can remember *all* their names."

"Now I know you're teasing."

"I think one is enough, don't you?"

"You're probably right. I'm a possessive bastard. I'm not sure how I'd react to more than one of these fuckers."

"You won't ever need to worry about that." As I looked up at him, Alex leaned down and softly pressed his lips against mine.

"I love you, Nat. So fucking much!" he murmured against my lips before going in for a deeper kiss.

My body began to burn slowly from the inside as our tongues collided rapidly against each other. Why did our bedroom have to be so far away? Right now, all I wanted to do was rip Alex's clothes off and ride him until the sun came up in the morning.

"Pool house?" he growled against my lips, quickly gripping my butt and lifting me off the ground.

"W...what?" I knew what he meant despite my question, and my insides began to quiver.

"I want you naked in the pool house." All I could do was groan in response as he pushed the door open with his foot.

Once it closed behind us, we were both in a crazy race to get each other undressed. If it hadn't been for my underwear, Alex would have gotten me naked first.

We both stood there drinking in each other's bodies. My mouth was watering at the sight of his growing erection. The electric pulse in the air seemed to pull us together without us even realizing it.

Within seconds, Alex grabbed me and pinned me against the wall. His hips ground into me, pinning me in place. He held my wrists above my head, kissing down my neck.

"This isn't going to be soft, Straight Lace. I want to ram my cock so hard inside you that you see stars."

"Do it!" I gasped, feeling the tip of his cock tease my clit. Tiny shocks of pleasure started to pulse around my body.

"You want this?" he snarled, teasing me more, pushing inside me ever so slowly before quickly pulling out.

"Ugh! Yes, I want it. Fuck me! Please."

"Oh Baby, that would be my pleasure." He smirked as he rammed himself deeply inside me. "I love how fucking wet you get for me!" Grabbing my legs, he used them as leverage to fuck me hard.

"Shit! Yeah, just there," I moaned, digging my nails into his back.

"I want these, too." He gripped one of my breasts roughly, sucking my nipple into his mouth and swirling his tongue around and around. It was such a glorious torture. "Are you going to cum loudly for me?"

"Fuck! Yeah, if you keep doing that." I was already building. Honestly, I wasn't sure how much longer I could hold it.

"Give it to me, Baby. I want it all. I want to feel your body tremble around my cock." At his words, I came undone. My body erupted with the most intense orgasm of my life.

"Fuck, yes! That's it." I looked up in my haze to watch his face as he came. I'd never tire of seeing Alex lose his shit while he was inside me.

CHAPTER SIX

"Did you drink any whiskey earlier?" I asked, watching Alex as he finished getting dressed in the pool house.

"No. I couldn't bring myself to take a single sip. I didn't want to disappoint you." My heart began to hammer hard in my chest. Did I affect him that much?

"I'm sorry for running out on you earlier. I know you worry."

"You needed space, I get it now. I only got all worked up because I was worried about you. Next time you need to let me know what's going on in that beautiful head of yours, Straight Lace. Don't leave me hanging like that. You know my mind is fucked up. I'll be imagining all sorts of scenarios."

"I will, I'm sorry." Moving towards him, I wrapped my arms around his waist. "We can't let David get to us. That's what he wants. You don't know him like I do."

"Why don't we go up to our bedroom, it's late? You can tell me all about what he's like. Don't worry, though. He's not going to touch us, Baby." Alex was so sincere as he gazed into my eyes. I couldn't *not* believe him.

"Why are you so afraid of people leaving you? Where does that fear come from?" It was a bold question, but I wanted to understand him.

"I'm not sure. People have left me since I was a kid. Maybe it's that."

"You mean when your mum left?" I watched his body stiffen at my words. This was uncomfortable for him.

"That's not a memory I like to relive. I don't talk about either of my parents. They're both gone, so what's the point?"

"They were your parents, though, Alex. They are part of you."

"My father sure is. He liked a drink, too. That's what killed him, you know." Okay, I didn't know that! Alex must have kept that from the media. I knew he'd died about five years ago, but the press stated it was a heart attack. "The bastard deserved it! He never supported mum through her cancer. Can we change this fucking subject now please? I don't want to think about either of them anymore!" Stress was radiating off his body.

"It's okay. I won't mention them again," I soothed. "Let's just go upstairs."

It was a clear night when we walked out onto our balcony. Alex was calmer now that I'd dropped the subject of his parents.

"I bet I'll get a great view from my telescope tonight," I mused, looking up at the thousands of twinkling lights in the sky. "Maybe I'll finally find a star we can name." Alex had taken to stargazing with me. Secretly, I knew he enjoyed it—even if it wasn't as manly as racing cars or jamming with legendary musicians.

"I'd buy you a star if you wanted it that much." I turned to see Alex slipping out of his shirt that he hadn't long put back on. I'd been around him for over a year so you'd think that I'd be used to his drool worthy body by now, but I wasn't. I still did a silly girly giggle that all his groupies did when he stripped.

"Are you giggling at me?" He quirked a perfect eyebrow.

"I'm laughing at myself and the effect you still have on me."

"Oh, really?" He looked amused at my confession. "Come over here and I'll affect you some more. We can stargaze later." That was an offer I couldn't refuse. It would help calm his mind too.

"Remind me what we're doing again?" Shane had driven Alex and me to the outskirts of Hollywood Hills. "What could you possibly get for Diego out here? There are just a few random houses." I paused. "Shit! Are you buying him a house for his birthday?"

"I don't love the fucker *that* much, Nat," Alex snorted, removing his sunglasses. "We're almost there." I was so confused. There was nothing here. If he wasn't buying Diego a house, I had no idea what we were doing out here. "I love it when you pout." I wasn't even aware that I was pouting. "You'll find out soon enough. Remember, we're only buying one, though." I frowned, which made Alex laugh out loud before kissing my forehead.

The moment we got out of the SUV, I knew what he meant. I could hear the barks before I even saw what breed they were.

"You're getting him a *puppy!*" I gasped, clapping my hands with excitement.

"Not quite. All these dogs need rehoming. Diego and I found out about the place through some contacts in the UK a few years ago who specialize in this particular breed."

"Are they all dalmatians?" Alex nodded. "Diego will freak if we get him his *own* Dalmatian!" He'd been obsessed with the breed since he was a kid thanks to Disney. Now that I thought about it, I was sure Diego had mentioned this place before. He'd done a fashion charity fundraiser for them.

"He's given so much to this place and Dalmatians in general. I think he deserves his own," Alex pointed out, ringing the doorbell.

"Do you think Diego has the patience to look after a dalmatian?"

"He needs something constant in his life. I think a dalmatian will fill that need."

"I hope you're right," I chuckled as the door opened. A tall, biker-type guy stood before us with a long grey beard.

"Ernie, my man!" Alex greeted him like an old friend. "How's Maggie?"

"She's almost finished with chemo. It's all looking good." Ernie turned to look at me. "And who is this beautiful lady?"

"This is Nat," Alex replied proudly. I could tell he wanted to put his arms around me, but he controlled himself. "She's my PA. Has been for almost a year."

"I thought I saw Millie doing a talk show a few weeks back." Ernie scratched his head. "I wondered if I was just seeing things in my old age."

"Yeah, she lives in New York now. She's made quite a celebrity of herself." Alex turned towards me. "Ernie and Maggie have given their whole lives to looking after this breed. They do so much for them."

"A lot of it we couldn't do without your donations." Ernie chuckled to himself and then turned to me. "The things this man has done for us. Diego has been wonderful, too. I've known the two of them for over ten years."

"I know Diego will do anything for the breed and Alex is just amazing," I grinned. Alex stood there looking as innocent as he could. How large was his heart?

"Are you ready to see the dally's? They're all out back. I've put the rehomed ones in the house."

We walked outside and it was dalmatian heaven. There had to be at least fifteen excited dogs running around playing with each other.

"Oh. My. God. It's just like the film!" The excitement was evident in my voice. All Alex could do was laugh at me as I sank to my knees and all the Dalmatians started to run my way. "How are we going to pick just one?" I giggled, allowing myself to be covered in doggy kisses.

"I was thinking a male. That should narrow it down." Alex knelt down to stroke one of the smaller dalmatians. "What about this one? Is he male?"

"He's quite a character, that one," Ernie chuckled. "He loves chewing shoes." Alex and I both looked at each other. A dog that chewed shoes was perfect for Diego. I was checking out the heart-shaped spot over his left eye when it dawned on me—he had one blue and one brown eye.

"He's perfect! Look at that unique face!"

We looked at the other dogs in the yards, but none seemed as perfect as the shoe chewer. "We'll take him." Alex decided, pointing to him. "I think he's made for Diego. I'll get Shane to pick him up next week once you've done all the relevant checks." Alex handed over some cash to Ernie.

"Alex, this is too much money."

"Keep the rest, Ernie. You deserve it." Would I ever get used to Alex's softer side? It annoyed me that the press never portrayed the goodness in him. There was so much more to him than his career as a musician and the bad-boy persona they so often portrayed. Alex really took care of those that had been there for him in the past.

"Maybe we should name the dog before we give him to Diego," Alex mused while we made our way back to the house. "He's going to think of some shitty name like Prince or Pongo."

"Those aren't bad names." I laughed.

"I was thinking he looked like a Ralph. At least it's an actual name." I had to admit, I liked it. "I'll get Shane to get a blue bow for next week."

"You're so good to people, did you know that? What you did for Ernie...you're amazing."

"I have the money and I don't like watching good people struggle. I want to do more to help."

"You're doing enough." I sighed, resting my head on his shoulder.

Diego fell in love with Ralph the moment he laid eyes on him. He cried for almost five hours. I'd never seen him so happy. Having a dog around the house lightened everyone's mood, too. Diego took to caring for Ralph really well. He went to dog school, learning all about the needs of the breed, which included lots of exercise and a raw feed diet. Ralph needed a lot of attention and Diego was all too happy to give it. To be honest, they formed an unbreakable bond really quickly and it was wonderful to watch.

With the PR for Steel Roses starting to fall into place, it meant Alex and I were in regular meetings with David.

"The press conference will be in a month's time. By then, I want you and the rest of the band to be like a well-oiled machine. I don't care about all the shit that's gone on in the past." I could see Alex's anger begin to flare before David had even finished talking.

"Do you have any idea what you're asking?" Alex was trying to keep calm, but the tension was seeping into his voice. "Have you had this *chat* with the rest of the band?"

"I don't need to. *You* are the front man. Grow a pair of balls and deal with it."

"Fucking *deal* with it?!" Alex was out of his chair, towering over David. "Who the *fuck* do you think you are?" I stood up and gently touched his shoulder, silently urging him to sit back down. This was the outburst David wanted.

"I'm your boss, Alex, and you'll be wise to remember that." You couldn't help but notice the sneer in his voice. "I have the power to make or break you. Don't ever forget it!"

"You're wrong!" The words were out of my mouth before I could stop them. I wasn't about to let David think he had any power over Alex. "You're trying to say you have power over a legendary rock star. Do you know how stupid you sound?"

"This has nothing to do with you. You're just the little PA, Natasha!" David was trying to undermine me.

"You'd like to think that's all she is to me, wouldn't you?" Alex's voice was so controlled as he took my hand in his. "Nat is what this is all about. I've got you all worked out! You had your chance but you couldn't see what was standing right in front of you. Be the better man and walk away, David. This isn't a battle you're going to win."

"Once you've tired of her, I'll be the one to put her back together again. When have you ever had a healthy relationship?" David always liked to have the last word, but I had the feeling that he wasn't going to win this time.

"She makes me want to work towards one. I've met countless women over the years, but none have captured me the way she has. I don't need to sit here and explain to you what she means to me. Nat already knows." I smiled softly back at him as he gazed at me. "I suggest we get back to tour related business before you embarrass yourself any further, David. If you carry on, I may even have to put a complaint in about you. I'd hate for you to lose your job, but don't think for one moment that I wouldn't be able to make that happen!"

"I think we're done for the day." David glared at us before turning his attention to his computer screen. I'd seen that look before. He was backing down for the time being, at least.

"That fucker is starting to test my patience." Alex sighed as we made our way down in the elevator.

"He's just trying to get under your skin and get a reaction from you."

"He'll get a fucking reaction if he carries on. My fist in his smug face!" I tried to hide my smirk. "I fucking *mean* it, Straight Lace!"

"I know you do, that's why I'm smiling. It would be an easy fight for you, though. I'm not sure it would be worth it."

"It would be worth it just to see him with a black eye." Alex had a point, but I knew the trouble he would get into if he actually did it.

"The best way to get to David is to ignore him. You have bigger things to worry about anyway. Rehearsals start soon." Alex nodded sadly, moving towards me to kiss my forehead. "It will be fine," I whispered into his chest.

"You're too hopeful sometimes, Straight Lace. It always gets worse before it gets even remotely better."

"You're off with your timing again!" Matt snarled, throwing his guitar down. "The drugs have destroyed your brain cells!"

"Man, Alex was in time. You kept changing the fucking riff! That's not what we decided on." Cody was trying to reason with Matt.

It was week two of rehearsals and the tension between Matt and Alex hadn't gotten any better. Rock Records had hired a recording studio that came complete with a rehearsal room. It was only an hour from Alex's LA home, which meant we didn't have to stay in a hotel like the rest of the band. The PR for the reunion concert was slowly building, and once the band had done their first live performance in over ten years, the world tour would be announced and the tickets would go on sale. That's when the media circus would *really* begin.

"Masen, what do you think? Was Alex off again?" I could see what Matt was doing. He was trying to divide the band. The look on Alex's face told me he was ready to throw in the towel for the day, and I didn't blame him. He couldn't get anything right in Matt's eyes. These last two weeks had been anything but easy.

"He seemed fine to me, Matt. I think you're being a little over critical." Masen rubbed his temple. They'd been practicing for hours; everyone must have been tired.

"Over fucking critical? Do you have any idea how much is riding on this tour?!" Matt was losing it. "It has to be *perfect!*"

Diego stood up from his seat in the corner of the room and started to walk towards them. "Maybe we should call it a night?" he suggested once he'd reached them. "Emotions are still flying high, and I think a good night's sleep would help all of you."

"Diego has some guts," Naomi, the tour manager, whispered in my ear. "Honestly, I still think getting Alex and Matt in a boxing ring would help." She'd managed the band in the early days, and was keen to see how they were getting on in preparation for the world tour that was now only six months away.

"You'd want to charge for tickets, though," I teased. She sniggered in agreement before we both turned back towards the raised voices. I liked Naomi—she and I had a similar sense of humor.

"Who the fuck asked you, Diego?" Matt snarled, getting in his face.

"Don't make me bitch slap you, Matt! You know I've done it before!" Diego stood tall in his heels. Matt's aggressive tone didn't even faze him. "You need to calm the fuck down and stop taking everything out on Alex. Don't you think this is difficult for him, too? Neither of you want this, but at least he's manned up and is dealing with it!"

"We knew whose side you took years ago, Diego. You don't have to keep defending him!"

"Alex is my *best friend*! No one else gave a fuck about him when all the shit blew up. He could have died if it weren't for…"

"Diego…" Alex cautioned him by patting him on the back,

but his worried eyes met directly with mine.

"He's being a fucking *cock*! He needs to know what you went through!" I'd never seen Diego so wound up before. The tension was radiating from his body in waves.

"What *he* went through!?" Matt dropped his guitar. "Oh, I forgot...everything is *always* about Alex! He's the frontman, after all. He can do whatever the fuck he wants, can't he? I'm fucking done for the day!" With that he stormed off, slamming the door behind him.

"How the fuck are we going to make this work?" Masen sighed from behind his drums. "We've got eight weeks to get this shit right before our first live performance." The band's debut comeback performance was on Milly's evening chat show in two months. It was the perfect set up, really. Having all the old gang together again. If only they could get on.

"We could just get a new lead guitarist," Cody teased, turning to wink at me. "What do you think, Nat?"

"The fans might get a little upset," I snorted. "But I do see your logic."

"Nat's right. We can't disappoint the fans. I do love your idea, though, Cody," Alex chuckled.

"I can't see this getting better any time soon." Masen stood up. "I think we need to talk it out tonight. Come to some sort of agreement. Matt is being unreasonable. We all see it, even if he doesn't."

"Will Matt even listen, though?" Cody didn't sound very hopeful.

"He better. We'll make him if we have to." Alex took a deep breath and I felt my own catch in my throat. "Let's get this over with then. There's no time like the present."

None of the band looked optimistic as they left the room.

CHAPTER SEVEN

Whatever had happened after rehearsals last night had worked. The band seemed to be trying to get on this morning and I couldn't quite believe the chills that were running down my spine as I stood listening to Steel Roses rehearse my favorite song.

'Wings of an Angel' was such a poetic tune. I was fifteen the first time I'd heard it, and to this day, no song had ever captured me in the same way. Even knowing the real muse behind the lyrics didn't faze me. It may have been written about Vanessa, but the words still spoke to me. Loving Alex as deeply as I do, I knew all about that fear of losing someone...of not being enough to hold that person; I knew if I wasn't careful, they could slip through my fingers.

Alex's voice was so raw and emotional as he sang. I leaned against the wall in the far corner of the room trying to act unfazed, but I was failing...miserably.

"He's amazing, isn't he?" Diego whispered. "I love it when he gets this immersed in a song."

"I have no words." I couldn't keep my eyes off Alex. His were closed, but I could tell he was feeling every single word he was singing.

"Even to this day he has no idea just how talented he is." I nodded, taking in every line of Alex's face and etching this moment into the back of my mind. He'd played such a large part of my past and now he was my future. That was a lot for a *groupie* like me to take in. When I was younger, of course I'd fantasized about being here, but to have it come true...it was all so surreal. How did I get here again?

"What did you think?" Alex was beaming as he stood in front of Diego and me once he'd finished the song. "I think the timing is getting much better."

"You were incredible. I've never heard the gritty tone in your voice so close and personal before." As I listened to myself, I realized how much I sounded like a crazed fan. Alex was my boyfriend. Why did I suddenly feel so different?

"Oh, I'm sure you have," he teased, winking at me before turning back towards the band. "How about we break for an hour?" They all nodded and started to collect their belongings. "Are you hungry?" He was talking to me again, but all I could do was nod. "There's a burger place down the road. I'll get Shane to drive us." I followed him wordlessly towards the SUV. "You're really quiet," he mused once we were in the back of the car. "Have I done something wrong?" He asked, offering me a malteser from the second pack I'd seen him eat today.

"Why would you think that?" I smiled, scooting closer to him and taking a malteser from his pack. His arms automatically wrapped around me.

"The silent treatment is usually because you're pissed off at something."

"You haven't done anything wrong," I giggled. "I'm in awe of you, that's all."

"You are? I thought you got all of that out of your system when we met?"

"So did I." I sighed, giving him a big smile.

"I was a total dick, remember?" Giving me a lazy smirk, he moved a little closer. "Or did you really want my dick the moment you met me?"

"Jerk!" I teased, nudging him playfully. "You know that was the last thing on my mind when we first met!"

"Yeah, you were such a challenge, Straight Lace. I never thought I'd get in your pants."

"I'm more than aware of the *challenge* you thought I was." I snorted, moving to rest my head on his shoulder. "You sang my favorite Steel Roses song earlier."

"Which one?"

"Wings of an Angel." I felt him go rigid against me. "It's okay. I know that most of it was inspired by Ness, but that doesn't make it any less beautiful."

"No, that's not it." I moved to look up at him when I heard the astonishment in his voice. "Back in the early days Ness was the one I thought about while performing it, but those words now...all I see when I sing it is you. With you, the words hold more meaning than they ever did with Ness." My mouth had gone dry and I was sure I'd forgotten to breathe. "It's because I know you're mine. I had to share Ness. I thought what she and I had was love but I was fucking wrong." As a single happy tear trickled down my face, I had a beautiful sense of clarity. Alex and I were strong enough for the world tour. With a love as powerful as ours, there was no way we could fail.

"If you don't calm down, I'm not letting you in." Liv was hyperventilating at the front door of Alex's Hollywood home. She'd been pestering me to allow her to visit for months, and I couldn't put it off any longer.

"I...I think I need a brown paper bag! Nat, I'm not sure I can breathe!"

I laughed, shaking my head at her.

"I'm being fucking *serious!*"

"It's just Alex and Cody. It's not like the whole band is here, Liv. Get a grip," I teased.

"Cody is here too?!" she screeched, moving to lean against the door frame before she fell over. "You didn't tell me that!"

"I didn't know he'd be staying. Rehearsals went well this morning and Cody wanted to go over a few riffs with Alex."

"Are you telling me they are both jamming together in this house at this moment?" Liv looked like she was going to pass out when I nodded. "Holy shit!"

I was still giggling at her when Shane came up behind her, holding her luggage.

"Are you going to stand outside all day or go in?" he teased, making Liv jump and spin around to see who was behind her.

"Fuck, don't do that! I thought you were Alex!" She took a deep breath, then added, "I don't mind carrying my own bags."

"That would be ungentlemanly of me, now, wouldn't it?" Shane gave her a cheeky wink before making his way inside. I noticed Liv giving Shane the once over, and could tell by her face that she fancied him.

"Shane's a sweetheart," I commented as she came out of

her little daze.

"Yeah, yeah, he is," she sighed. "Shit, why am I freaking out so much? You're dating Alex! I'm just meeting him." In the corner of my eye, I noticed that Alex was making his way up the hallway towards us.

"Alex isn't *that* amazing, Liv. You'll realize he's an asshole the moment you meet him."

"Why are you dating him, then?" she snorted.

"I ask her the same question daily," Alex butted in. "It's lovely to finally meet you, Liv. Are you coming in or are you sleeping on the porch?" Liv's face was a picture when she saw who was speaking to her. Her eyes widened, and she swallowed hard, taking a deep breath to try and answer him.

"I...um...I...I'll come in...th-thank you." She almost stumbled as she stepped towards him. I'd never seen her look so star-struck.

"How was your flight?" I asked, trying to help Liv snap out of the daydream she was clearly having about *my* boyfriend. I couldn't blame her, though. Alex looked sexy as hell in his faded jeans and tight, black V-neck top.

"Um...it was good, thanks." She couldn't keep her eyes off Alex. This could get embarrassing.

"Did Nat tell you about the party we're having this weekend?" I widened my eyes at Alex. What party? I knew nothing about it.

"N...No?" Liv moved her stare towards me for a brief second.

"Yeah, we're having a pool party and the whole band will be here." Oh God, I hoped he was joking.

"You mean you'll...? You'll all be...?"

"Practically naked?" Alex finished Liv's sentence for her, and in that moment I knew he was teasing.

"Oh, I...um..."

"He's messing with you, Liv," I snorted, slapping his arm. "Can you give us half an hour so I can show Liv her room? You seem to be having an effect on her!"

"Of course. I'll let you sort her out." He grinned, pecking my lips and slapping my butt before walking off with a devilish grin.

"Fuck! He just kissed you and slapped your arse. You lucky *bitch!*" Liv had the biggest smile on her face. "Taking away his hotness and rock god status, he is making you happy, right?" This was why she was my best friend. I hadn't seen her in almost nine months, yet I knew she cared and was generally happy for me.

"He makes me more than happy," I sighed, and with that Liv hugged me tight.

Once I'd helped her unpack and settle into her room, I started to show her around. She seemed calmer now, which was a good thing. From experience, I knew it was a lot to take in. I remembered my first impressions of the Hollywood Hills house.

"There's not going to be a Steel Roses pool party, right?" Liv asked, following me towards the kitchen.

"No, Alex was teasing you. There's still a bit of tension with the band. I'm not sure you'll get to meet them all on this trip."

"You mean Matt is still being a dick?" I wasn't surprised that Liv had guessed which member was being difficult. The press had been making up their own stories for weeks, but none were that far from the truth.

"You could say that."

Mary was in the kitchen. We were doing quick introductions when Diego wandered in quickly followed by his shadow, Ralph.

"Olivia, darling! It's so good to finally meet you." Diego had interrupted so many of Liv's and my Skype calls that the two of them knew each other pretty well already.

"It's lovely to meet you, too. Awww, your dog is gorgeous!" Liv cooed over Ralph until Shane walked in without a shirt on. That was something Shane didn't do very often. Straight away, Diego and I realized what was going on. Liv and Shane were both giving each other the eye.

"Trying to impress someone, Shane?" Diego quirked his eyebrow at him.

"Me?" Shane pretended to look shocked. "No. I'm just going to have a dip in the pool."

"Through the kitchen?" Diego questioned.

"I wanted a drink first. Jeez, stop interrogating me!" With that, he walked out towards the pool area. Liv's eyes followed him until he dived into the pool.

"You can go for a swim if you want." I smirked at her.

"Maybe later," she blushed, looking at me. Liv never blushed. "Where are Alex and Cody?"

"In the studio. They'll come out when they're done. Don't worry, you'll meet Cody before he leaves," I joked. "Why don't we chill out by the pool area? You need to try and stay awake through the jet lag, anyway."

"I'm too excited to sleep, I'll be fine."

"Yeah, let's have a few drinks outside. You can fill me in on the naughty things Nat has done in the past," Diego interrupted with a wink at Liv.

"That will take a few weeks," she laughed, following us outside.

It was nice having my best friend come stay for a few weeks. Once she'd gotten over the fact that Alex was just a person, it was much easier. She could relax and be the Liv I knew and loved.

"You need to tell me about David!" Liv whispered. "Did he follow you to Rock Records?" Alex had gone to a PR meeting with the rest of the band, so besides Liv and me, it was only Diego and Mary left in the house.

"I'm hoping he didn't, but it's been a difficult few months. He's trying to make Alex's life miserable."

"The bastard! Can't Alex just fire him?"

"I wish it was that simple." I began to play with the pen in front of me.

"What's up, Nat?"

"I'm worried about how far David will go to make trouble for Alex and me. Alex has no idea how underhanded David can be."

"I've only known Alex for a week, but I'd say he can look after himself. He worships you, Natty. He's not going to let anything destroy that."

"You can tell all that in just a week?"

"It was easy to see after a few *days*. The love radiates off the pair of you. It's quite sickening, actually." I shook my head, smiling. "Joking aside, seeing you so happy...it's amazing. You two are so right for each other. And I love how you put him in his place, too."

"He secretly likes my assertive side."

"I'm sure he does!" She winked conspiratorially.

"I didn't mean it in that way, Liv. You're such a whore!"

"I've known you too long to think you meant it any other way, Nat!" She did have a point, but I didn't want her knowing she was right.

"It's going to be difficult for us when the world tour starts."

"In what way?"

"Every way. The band doesn't know about us, and David put Alex on a girlfriend bann for the entire tour."

"Wait! What? Can he even do that?"

"It's in the contract. At the time we didn't know it was David that had written it. I feel like everything he's doing is to get back at me for picking Alex and not him."

"That does sound like David. What a fucking prick!"

"I've told Alex the best way to deal with him is to not rise to his games."

"I'm guessing Alex didn't like the idea?" I nodded, sighing to myself. "You know what? You worry too much. If anyone can take David on, it's *Alex Harbour*! Everything will be fine."

"I know that, Liv, but it doesn't keep me from worrying. Alex has enough to deal with when it comes to the tour. I don't like adding to his problems."

"Nat, you're not a *problem*. You're his *girlfriend*!" Shaking her head at me, Liv folded her arms across her chest. "There is nothing that man wouldn't do for you. Relax and enjoy the ride."

"You're being dirty again. I can tell." I giggled, nudging her playfully.

"When am I not?" she snorted. I was going to miss Liv

when she went back home.

"You can ask her to stay, you know. I'm sure I could find her a job." I looked at Alex in disbelief. "What?"

"I only said that I would miss my best friend when she went home. You don't have to offer her a job, Alex!"

"I want to make you happy, Straight Lace. She was good company for you when I was busy with tour stuff."

"But a job? Really? What would you hire her for?"

"I don't know. She could be your assistant?"

"The personal assistant's assistant?" I tried not to laugh. It sounded ridiculous.

"I think the title has a certain ring to it, actually."

"You're insane! Do you realize that?" Alex gave me a lazy smile before pulling me down so I was straddling him.

"Your workload has doubled in the last few months. I don't like all the extra hours you've been working."

"But I...."

"No buts. Just ask her. Even if it's only temporarily until Steel Roses go on tour." My rock star was impossible sometimes.

Of course when I asked Liv, she jumped at the chance. I'm not sure if she was more excited about staying in Hollywood longer or still being able to see Shane.

The two of them had become very close in the two weeks she'd been here. Liv had been almost as unlucky as me when it came to men. Shane was a decent, caring person, though, and I really hoped things were progressing in the way I wanted them to.

"Will I be able to still stay here?" Liv asked, bouncing around like an excited school girl.

"I'll have to ask Alex, but I can't see it being an issue. Maybe Shane will let you share with him," I teased, pushing her gently.

"Oh stop! If it's not you making comments, it's Diego." Liv began to blush. "Shane is a really nice guy."

"I agree with you, Liv, and I think it's wonderful that the two of you are getting close."

"You do?"

"Of course I do! Why wouldn't I?"

"He's head of Alex's security. I feel like I'm intruding in the life you've made for yourself here. If you don't want me to stay and take this job, I'll understand." Was that how she really felt? I loved having her around!

"Alex knows what you mean to me. You *are* part of my life, Liv. You're my best friend. I want you to stay as long as you want to!"

"Really?" she beamed. When I nodded, Liv hugged me tightly. "I do really like Shane, Nat."

"I know you do," I whispered into her ear. "He likes you, too." Okay, Shane hadn't told me that, but there was no harm in playing matchmaker. I happened to think they were perfect for each other. Besides, it gave me something to think about other than Steel Roses going on tour—or David 'Asshole' Barclay.

CHAPTER EIGHT

"You have that worried look on your face again." Diego smirked. "Relax, will you? Milly isn't *that* scary."

"I feel like she's always judging me when I'm with Alex. I should be used to it having met her a few times now but I'm not."

"Milly has everyone on edge. That's just her. Don't worry, Baby Cakes." That was easy for him to say. Steel Roses was *hours* away from its first live performance in over twenty years. As a band, they had decided to do it on Milly's popular talk show. Alex was a nervous wreck and I wasn't much better!

"Where are they?" I heard Milly's voice before I saw her. Diego and I were currently sitting in the green room while the band was going over their cues with the set manager that worked for Milly's show. She appeared at the door looking as glamorous as ever. Hollywood had been good to Milly; she was glowing with success. "What are you two doing hiding away here?"

"We're giving the band some space." Diego replied, getting up to hug her. "How have you been? You look smoking hot! Which designer is this? I love it! I wonder if they have it in my size?" He pulled at her tight red dress. Next to these two, I felt utterly underdressed. They were the epitome of fashion.

"How are you holding up, Nat?" Milly turned to me after

they'd finished their catch up. "You look as nervous as Alex."

"I think we'll both be glad once this is over. It's a huge step for the band." She nodded warmly. "Do you think Matt will behave on live TV?"

"Oh, I can control that asshole if he starts. I'll be on my guard, don't worry. I've told him that I won't allow any arguing or fighting on my talk show!" The look on Milly's face gave me some peace of mind. She cared for Alex. She wasn't going to let anything happen to him.

"Your show is amazing, by the way. Alex is so proud of you."

"Thanks. It's taken off faster than I thought. I owe so much to Alex." She looked over at Diego. "I've been trying to get Diego on board as the show's fashion expert." My eyes widened. He hadn't told me about that. "He's being stubborn as always."

"You never said anything!" Diego looked down at the floor as I scolded him.

"It's about timing. I'm not leaving Alex right now. He needs all of us." My eyes softened. I understood that better than anyone. Milly accepted his explanation with a nod. "It's not that I'm not flattered at your offer, Mills. I'll consider it one day."

"Whatever, Bitch." She winked. "I think we've left the band alone long enough. Let's go and see what those dickheads are doing."

The guys looked quite calm as they walked around the studio. Alex had his hands in his pockets and I could tell he was trying to take everything in. The tension was radiating off him in waves and it was making me extremely nervous. Would Matt intentionally mess up the performance or start an argument live on air? I didn't know him well enough to know if he would do that or not, but I had the faith that Milly would handle the situation if he tried anything.

Alex turned and gave me a sexy, sly smile. My insides melted every time he did that.

"Are you finished with them?" Milly asked her set manager. "I'd like to take these assholes to lunch."

"You've got to work on your affectionate tone, Milly. That was fucking awful!" Mason laughed, shaking his head at her.

"I can call you cock suckers whatever I want!" she teased. "Come on, let's eat. I'm famished."

Milly took us all to a swanky sushi restaurant not too far from the studio. New York was the only town I'd visited that was just like the movies. The streets weren't pathed in gold, it just had an edge to it. The air even tasted different somehow. It stood out for its own reasons. That was one of the things I loved about this city. The rawness and familiarity as you took in the large skyscrapers and iconic buildings was enough to take your breath away.

"Are you seeing anyone at the moment, Matt?" Milly asked, taking a sip of her wine. The conversation between all of us had been flowing quite well until that comment.

"I've been meaning to ask Alex the same question for a while now. He always has a chick hanging off his arm, yet I haven't seen him with a single piece of ass since we started talking again." I swallowed hard, turning to look at Alex. He was as calm as ever. How did he hold himself together like that?

"I've decided to concentrate on the tour. I don't want to be distracted by anything or anyone."

"Bullshit. Someone will catch your eye. The fans don't call you 'jackhammer' for nothing," Matt sneered. "Hopefully you'll catch some disease that will make your cock shrivel up and fall off this time around."

"Matt," Milly cautioned, "don't be such a fucking dick. People *can* change. You've spent the last ten years avoiding Alex, so how the fuck would you know anyway!?"

"You think he's *changed*?" Matt's eyes began to burn with fury. "I didn't think he'd be able to fool *you*, Milly. Alex will always be a selfish cunt! That will never change. *Never!* The moment we go on tour he'll be knee deep in pussy. You just wait and see!"

"You're making that judgement from twenty years ago, Matt. I can assure you that I'm *not* that person anymore. You need to fucking let all this shit go before it starts to eat you from the inside." Alex remained cool and in control. Deep down, he wanted to help Matt. They both needed to heal from the bitter past they shared.

"Are you telling me that I need to let Ness go, too?! *All* my good memories of her were gone the moment I found out you'd been fucking her behind my back. You made me *hate* the only woman I've ever loved because you couldn't keep it in your fucking pants!"

"It wasn't just about sex. I've explained this!"

"Of course it was just about sex. You're incapable of loving anyone!" Matt slammed his beer bottle on the table. "You just wanted what was mine, you heartless bastard!"

"You really think I'm incapable of love?" Alex's gaze dropped from Matt and turned briefly towards me. His demeanor changed before he continued to speak. He was protecting both of us. "Think what you like, Matt. Your opinions have never mattered to me. The days of us being like brothers are long gone. I know that's my fault, but I refuse to carry this burden around anymore."

"Brother? Ha! What a joke." Matt's eyes darkened. "I wish you were capable of love, though." Everyone was silent at the table, listening intently. Alex looked confused, wondering what Matt was going to say next. "Do you want to know why?"

"You're going to tell me regardless, so please...carry on," Alex sighed, taking a sip of his water before slipping his hand in mine under the table.

"Then I'd be able to break you like you broke me. I'd pull you from your love piece by piece, *Brother.*" I swallowed hard at the deadly tone Matt used. Alex's hand gripped mine tighter. "I'd destroy you, the way you destroyed me."

"Matt, do you know how fucked up you sound?" Milly broke the silence around the table. "You're fucking threatening him in front of all these witnesses, you asshole."

"Do you think I give a fuck who hears? I want him to suffer like I did!"

"We're never going to get past this, are we?" Alex looked defeated.

"No!" Matt spat. In one swift movement, Alex stood up and walked out of the restaurant.

"I'll go after him," I muttered, standing up while arguments began to erupt around the table. Everyone was gunning for Matt.

Alex was leaning against the wall outside. I was surprised no one had noticed him yet. New York was buzzing with the news of the live Steel Roses performance later.

"Hey," I whispered, desperate to reach out for him.

"Let's get a taxi," he muttered quickly, taking my hand. I

didn't know what was going on until he pulled me into the back of the taxi and muttered a few words to the driver before his lips were hard against mine.

"Nothing makes more sense than this right now," he sighed, taking a breath before going in for another deep kiss.

The moment Alex shut our bedroom door, I was pushed face first against the wall. His hands ran hungrily over my body, pulling at my clothes. I braced myself by placing my hands on the wall above me.

"Do you have any idea how sexy you are?" he purred into my ear, sucking on my earlobe.

"N...no," I panted as his hands slipped up inside my top.

"You must have an idea. Look how crazy you make me!" Alex gripped my breasts firmly and I leaned against his strong chest. "Shall I make you cum against this wall?"

"Yes." I'd agree to anything in that moment. My body was burning for his touch.

"Mmm...maybe I should make you wait. Drive you crazy, like you do to me." I could hear the playful smile in his voice. "Then again, I'm not sure I want to wait to hear your moans." His hands moved down and slid into my shorts. "Oh, someone is ready to be played with." I could hardly focus on anything else as he began to rub my clit frantically. "Brace yourself. This is going to be quick." At his words, he inserted two of his fingers inside me and set a maddening pace.

It didn't take me long to explode around his fingers, and I slumped against his body as I fell into the abyss.

"I can't wait to sink my cock inside you, Straight Lace." I'd barely regained my thoughts before he moved me so I was bent over the couch. "That will do." Quickly, he pulled my panties down my legs and with one deep thrust he was inside me. "Fuck, Baby. That's it. Take my cock!"

My fingers dug into the arm of the couch as he continued his glorious torture. I knew this was what he needed. We both did. It was how we released our tension—how we reconnected in a world that at times made no sense to us.

"I don't want to cum yet." Alex pulled out just as I began to shudder again. "Fuck, Baby. I love the sounds you make when you cum." As I began to come around from my climax, Alex flipped me over and slowly sank back inside me. "This is going to be a slow build. I want to enjoy your pussy wrapped around my cock." Moving a hand down, he began to play with my clit gently. It was already sensitive from the previous orgasms. "Do you like that, Baby?"

"Ugh! Oh, God yes!! Yes!" I began to arch up towards him.

"No, slow. Feel my cock inside you." Closing my eyes, I began to concentrate on how Alex was making my body feel. When we climaxed it was almost as one.

"I *am* capable of loving you, Straight Lace. I don't care what Matt says," he whispered as he carried me to our bed.

"Alex, I know you are. Don't pay any attention to him." Caressing his face with my hand, I gazed into his clear, cool blue eyes.

"We have half an hour before we need to think about getting ready for the show. What can I do to you in that time?" He had a playful grin. There was a lot we could do in thirty minutes.

"Where did you two disappear to?" Diego eyed us

suspiciously as we walked into the studio a few hours later. "Milly was about to send out a search party."

"Nat left something at the hotel." Alex winked at me.

"Her panties probably," Diego muttered under his breath so only Alex and I could hear. I tried to hide my smirk as the others joined us.

"We thought you'd bailed on us," Cody called, concerned.

"No, I just needed some space to clear my head. You know how it is." Matt wouldn't even look at Alex as he spoke.

The band did their final sound check before they were taken to makeup. Diego had already worked on their outfits. Alex was wearing a sexy leather jacket and blue skinny jeans. The fans were going to go crazy when they saw him. It would be extremely difficult, but I knew I'd have to keep myself in check. I couldn't be the jealous girlfriend when no one knew about us.

"You should have brought Liv with you," Diego smirked. "She did put up a good argument about coming, after all."

"I don't think she minds holding down the fort back in LA. I couldn't watch her and Shane all over each other for another moment."

"You did good matchmaking there, Baby Cakes."

"I really hope I don't regret it."

"Does she know Shane had a soft spot for you when you started?"

"No. It was just a soft spot anyway. Nothing ever happened. I know he really cares about Liv."

"I can't promise that I won't let his little crush on you slip when I'm drunk. You know how I get."

"If you do, I'll give you a wedgie every day for a year!"

"Bitch! That's not fair!" Diego looked horrified and I

couldn't stop giggling. "I'll give you a wedgie right now if you don't stop laughing!"

"Oh, come on. That was funny."

"Have you seen the shorts I wear? I don't wear panties under them!"

"Then keep your mouth shut and you'll have nothing to worry about," I winked. Diego was so easy to wind up. I was getting as bad as Alex.

Once the studio began to fill up with people, I decided to join some of the crew outside. The hysteria was beginning to build. The fans were even queuing outside the studio, hoping for a glimpse of Steel Roses together again.

"I can't wait for the tour." I heard one crew member say. "I think Alex looks better now than in the early days. I really hope they record some new material."

"It's all a money spinner. The band hates each other. They'll do the world tour, make their millions, then never speak again," another commented.

"They might surprise us. Doing a world tour puts a lot of pressure on a band. They wouldn't have agreed if they all hated each other."

"Want to make a bet?" I had to laugh at the craziness that surrounded Alex. Strangers were betting on whether or not the band would stay together.

It was a clear, sunny day in New York. The gentle breeze tickled my hair as I stood, catching my breath.

"Um, are you Natasha?" A voice came from behind me. The young man standing in front of me must have only been eighteen. He cleared his throat before speaking again. "Milly would like to see you in her dressing room." I'd been dreading talking to Milly one on one since I'd arrived. With a deep breath I made my way to see her.

"Have you been avoiding me?" She quirked her eyebrow at me as I entered her dressing room.

"No, why would you think that?" My high pitched voice betrayed me.

"You've been glued to Diego's side since you arrived." She did have a point. I'd either been with Diego or Alex the entire time. "How is Alex really doing with all this? I honestly can't read him."

"He's taking it a day at a time. Matt definitely isn't making it easy for him."

"Has Alex filled you in on *all* the history between them?"

"Yes, I know everything." Milly looked at me in surprise. "Alex and I are very open with each other."

"That's really good, Nat. I'm pleased for both of you. You have no idea how long Alex has been waiting for you. I never thought he'd find the right match."

"How dangerous is Matt, Milly?" I had to ask and hope she'd be honest with me. She knew the band and their history like no one else.

"The years haven't been good to him. He's all bitter and twisted. I really wouldn't like to say. I have no idea what he's capable of these days."

"They've got to get through an entire year of touring! How am I supposed to support Alex through all of that?"

"You won't even have to think about it. Everything you do for him is so effortless. I've noticed. He's so much calmer when you're around. Oh if you had seen him in his youth when I was doing your job." Milly chuckled to herself, lost in an old memory.

"He was a wild cat, Nat. Uncontrollable. They *all* were. The world loved them and treated them like gods. Alex was never grounded until he met you. Once he did, he realized there is more to life than fame." I couldn't look her in the eyes as she spoke. Had Alex talked about me *that* much? "It's okay to be scared, too, Nat. It's a lot of pressure on both of you. The key is to talk to him and be honest. This tour will have rough times I guarantee. The groupies will drive you crazy. Just remember—he loves *you*." I nodded, stunned by her kind words. "Now, let's kick start this comeback tour, shall we? I think the world has been without Steel Roses long enough, don't you?" I had to smile in agreement. My inner teenager did a girly squeal. It was finally show time.

The band owned their performance, Alex knew how to make love to the camera as he sang. I was pretty sure every Steel Roses aficionado around the world was glued to their screen watching him—feeling as if he was singing just to them.

Matt even played it cool after the song. Milly sure knew how to conduct a live interview. It probably helped that she knew the band so well. By the time the show went off air, the crew was all cheering. Millie had just gotten her highest viewer count ever.

The hysteria over Steel Roses was back, and all it was going to do now was continue build.

CHAPTER NINE

Standing there watching Steel Roses rehearse in a large warehouse felt like a dream. It was days until they kick-started their world tour. The last few months hadn't been easy. Tension was high between Alex and Matt, but somehow they'd managed to set aside their differences when it came to the music. That was the only common factor they had. Alex reminded Matt of that daily.

"Can you believe this is happening right now?" Liv giggled in my ear. "We're getting our own private show."

"I know, right? How many nights did we dream about this?"

"Too many. We must be the luckiest bitches alive." I had to snort at that. Liv was right.

"What are you two giggling about?" Diego questioned, handing us both a bottle of beer. "You're not comparing Shane and Alex's dick sizes again, are you?"

"When have we ever done that?!" Liv laughed. "You're the one obsessed about dick size!"

"It's because he isn't getting any," I teased.

"Bitch, please!" Diego grinned. "I get plenty. Perhaps not as much as you, though. You were squealing like a whore for hours last night." I wasn't going to rise to his comment because I knew he had a point. It was the easiest way for Alex to let off steam from the stress of the tour. Not that I was complaining; I loved every moment of it. "And she's not even going to deny it. Liv, can you see what your friend has become?"

"I always knew she had it in her."

"She had a lot *in her* last night, that's for sure." Diego winked at me as my mouth fell open. These two clearly thought they were a comedy act. "What? It's the truth."

"Shut the fuck up!" I grinned. "I'm trying to listen." Pointing towards the stage, my eyes met with Alex. He gave me a cheeky wink as he grabbed the microphone stand. His rough, gravelly voice made me want to drop to my knees in worship.

"You're still thinking about his cock, aren't you?" Diego whispered in my ear. "He'll want to shove it up your butt tonight." I slapped him playfully. He was such a tart. "Have you done anal yet?"

"I wouldn't tell you even if we had!"

"You're no fun," he said with a pout.

Our attention was drawn towards the stage as Alex began to strum the chords to Wonderlust. He hadn't told me *that* was on their setlist! "Didn't he tell you?" Diego asked, noticing my stunned face. I hadn't even known the band were letting him play one of his solo songs! A single spot light fell on Alex. It could have been just the two of us in that arena for all I cared. The gentle strum of his guitar had my heart pounding in my chest as he began to sing our song. It didn't matter how many times I listened to this song, it always felt like I was hearing the lyrics for the first time. The thought that *any* man could love me the way Alex did still took my breath away and he wasn't just *any man*. He was my rock star!

"He's haunting when he plays this song," Liv sighed, resting her head on my shoulder. "He really loves you, Natty." All I could do was grin at her in agreement.

Alex looked lost in the song as he continued to sing. The passion burning from his lips made me yearn for him. Looking towards Matt, I noticed he was gazing in my direction. Quickly, I looked away, not wanting to draw any attention towards Alex and me.

A sinking feeling hit my stomach and I wasn't sure why. Matt wouldn't have been able to work out what was going on between Alex and me so soon, but we still had the whole tour to get through. I was going to have to be really careful.

The beat of the drums pounded hard in my chest. The screaming was deafening from where I stood at the side of the stage. Steel Roses fans had waited so long for this moment, and it had finally arrived. I could hardly believe I was right here, beside Alex, as he took his first step back into the limelight that had destroyed him all those years ago. He was clutching his legendary guitar, waiting for his cue. The tour was starting in Italy to kick off the European portion.

"You'll be fine," I whispered into his ear before kissing his neck. The rest of the band were on stage so I knew the contact was safe.

"Have you *heard* that crowd?" He tried to laugh it off but swallowed nervously. "I used to think I was born for this, but it fucked me up so bad the first time around. Do I really want to do this again?"

"You didn't have me standing by you then." The worry in

his eyes faded as he pulled me towards him. My body crashed painfully against his guitar, but I didn't care once his lips pressed softly against mine.

"Don't move from this spot, Straight Lace. I need to be able to see you while I'm on stage," he muttered, leaning back to look at me.

"I'm not going anywhere. I'll be right here." With a smile on his face, he finally let me go and moved to take his place on the center of the stage. The noise was unbelievable as a single spotlight fell on him. My heart whimpered at the sight. All the band interviews, live TV spots and tour rehearsals hadn't prepared me for this. It was as if I was watching him walk into an abyss. The stadium was so loud that the walls were starting to shake. It was all for him. How *was* I going to protect Alex from the hysteria that surrounded him this time around?

"How are we feeling tonight, Rome?" Alex asked the crowd. "Are you all ready to fucking rock this place?" The stadium answered with a massive roar. "Let's fucking get it on!"

Naomi, the tour manager, came to stand next to me and shouted in my ear. "What do you think of the show so far?" I'd been in a daze for the last half an hour, watching Alex from the corner of the stage. "He's fucking rocking it out there. I've never seen him look so at home!" She was right. The spotlight was where Alex belonged, strumming his guitar, sweat dripping down his face because he was giving his fans as much of himself as he could. My body began to tremble with want as I watched him.

A huge part of my life was on that stage. I was reliving my childhood again and I couldn't stop the single tear of happiness that fell down my face. As stupid as it sounded, I understood how every single Steel Roses fan was feeling at this moment in time. They were getting back a part of their life that they thought was gone forever. Steel Roses had always been an escape from the daily grind. They were a solace when you felt the world crashing down around you. They were a lifeline for these fans' and a faith that tomorrow would be a better day. I couldn't imagine how Steel Roses felt knowing that they held that kind of power over people.

"I saw you rocking out back here, Baby." Alex smirked while he was changing his guitar at the side of the stage. "It's sexy as hell. I feel like you should take your bra off so I can see your tits bounce a bit more, though."

"Do you want me to throw my bra at you on stage? I'm so turned on that I would if you wanted," I teased, licking my lips.

"Fuck, don't say shit like that! I'll end up with a hard on when I go back on stage."

"You're amazing out there." I'd never wanted to kiss him as much as in that moment. The look of satisfaction and pride on his face left me breathless. "They're waiting for you, Alex."

"Just one more second. I'm savoring this moment, Straight Lace." I looked at him confused. "Being on stage has never felt like this before." He was gazing down at my lips and the longing was easy to see. "I want to kiss you so fucking bad right now."

"Save it for later. When we're alone you can kiss me *anywhere*." I winked, touching his chest. "GO!" I giggled at the shocked expression on his face.

"You are in so much trouble," he called over his shoulder as he walked back towards the spotlight. I had to hold my legs together at his threat.

By the time the band was halfway through their encore,

my ears were ringing from the music and the crowd. It was exhausting just watching the show. I couldn't even imagine how the band must have been feeling.

The stage crew were busy hustling around the side of the stage, waiting for their cue to start moving the set. I decided to wait for Alex in his dressing room, sure he'd head there first once he got off stage.

I sat with a huge grin on my face, watching the door. I knew he'd be sweaty and totally fuckable when he walked through it.

Seconds turned into minutes. I was sure they'd be off stage by now. They were finishing their last song when I left. After fifteen minutes, I decided I'd waited long enough.

As I was walking down the corridor, I heard lots of noise coming from the green room. I walked in to find all the band surrounded by VIP groupies and a few members of the press taking photos.

"There she is!" My body jolted at the voice coming from behind me. Of course David would have to turn up *now.* This whole setup had him written all over it. "I thought you'd already left."

"I wouldn't miss this for anything." Forcing a smile, I turned to face him.

"Don't you just love how the groupies all want a piece of him? I bet this is eating you up inside." David was uncomfortably close, whispering in my ear. My eyes fell on Alex. He wasn't even looking around for me; he was too focused on his fans. I tried to hide the rejection in my eyes. He must have been buzzing since coming off stage. I would have been the furthest thing from his mind. Taking all this personally was the wrong thing to do, I knew that, but my mind was still racing. Shouldn't he have come to find me first? I was the one he loved, after all. No, I was being silly. Alex was taking time for his fans. It meant nothing. Putting myself in check, I took a deep breath and responded to David.

"It's a part he has to play, David. We're a lot stronger than you think!"

"You have too much faith in him, Nat. You have a habit of falling for the wrong men, don't you?"

"The only wrong man I fell for was you! To be honest, I'm having a job understanding why I fell for you in the first place."

"I wish you'd been this feisty when we were fucking. I like this side of you." He reached out to touch my cheek, but I was quicker, slapping him hard around the face.

"You lost the right to touch me long ago, David. Stay the fuck away from me," I spat, storming off.

All I wanted in that moment was to be wrapped in Alex's arms, but he was surrounded by so many people that I couldn't even see him properly. My chest tightened as my breath caught in my throat. I needed to get out of this room.

"Baby cakes, you're white as a sheet." Diego was by my side in seconds, wrapping his arms around me.

"I...I need some air," I gasped. In one swift motion, he picked me up and carried me outside.

The fresh air was soothing. I took the largest breath I could as Diego placed me on a bench. "What was that with you and David?" he asked.

Running my hands through my hair, I tried to compose myself. "I think he's out to break me."

"Hush now. Alex won't let that happen, Nat."

"He just did!" I couldn't keep the hurt from my voice. Tears began to gently trickle down my face. "I had to fend for myself and slap David!"

"Oh, Baby Cakes, don't... You're letting him win if you start doubting Alex. It was a fucking good slap you gave that prick, though. I know all of this isn't easy. The attention Alex gets has always been immense. You can't let it get to you. It's just a role he has to play. This is his job." Diego wrapped his arms tightly around me as I began to sob uncontrollably. I didn't want to break this way, but I'd been strong for so long I needed to let go. "Let's get you back to the hotel. We don't want anyone to see you like this, especially that cock sucker, David!" All I could do was nod. I was suddenly exhausted, both physically and emotionally. All I wanted was my bed so I could sleep for days until my feelings faded away in the wind.

I was curled up tight into a ball in the hotel room bed. Even in my sleep I didn't feel calm. Everything was flashing through my mind. What if I lost Alex? What if the fame swallowed him whole? How could insignificant little *me* ever be enough for him? All my life I'd protected my heart and now it was going to be destroyed. I would never recover from this.

"Straight Lace," Alex's sweet voice in my ear instantly calmed me. I felt my body begin to uncurl from its tight stance. "Wake up, Baby." He pulled me towards his chest and I breathed in his scent as I opened my eyes. "Diego said you weren't feeling too good. Are you okay?" What could I tell him? That I feared he was going to slip away from me and this was only day one of the tour? That I was hurt he didn't come and find me after the show to help me deal with David? How selfish would that make me?

"I'm sorry, I didn't drink enough water today and got light

headed. I didn't want you to worry, so I got Diego to bring me back to the hotel." Why was it so easy to lie to him? This was a side of myself I didn't like. "You were incredible on the stage tonight." Seeing him perform felt like a distant memory at the moment.

"The crowd was insane. I'd forgotten how good it felt being on stage with the band behind me. We're pure fucking magic." Touching my face, he gazed down at me. "I was worried when I couldn't find you once I got off the stage. How are you feeling now?"

"Tired," I whispered, fighting my tears. Alex hadn't put the lights in the room on, so I took comfort that if any tears fell, he wouldn't see them.

"I'll let you sleep then, Baby. I love you." Our lips gently brushed as he ran his fingers through my hair. When he left a part of me ached. Why didn't he just get into bed with me and sleep? I didn't even know what time it was, but before I could think anymore I'd gone back under.

I stretched as the sun crept in through the gap in the curtains. My body felt as if it had been asleep for days. Moving over to Alex's side of the bed, I found it empty. Had he even been to bed after the show last night?

My head didn't feel any better when I sat up. My problems still seemed to be weighing me down. If this was what life on the world tour was going to be like, I wasn't sure I wanted any part of it. But this was the first leg of a four leg tour! Shaking those thoughts from my head, I calmed myself. Last night was the *first* show; I had to allow for that.

Once I'd gathered my thoughts, I had a shower and made

myself presentable.

I wandered around, trying to find Alex. The penthouse was full of never ending rooms, but they all seemed to be empty. Thoughts were still consuming me. Why wasn't he in the bed when I woke up? Why couldn't I find him now? Had he gone out again after our chat last night? Alex calling my name broke me from my mind. It sounded like he was in the next room.

"There you are." He smiled warmly at me as he walked through the door. "I didn't want to have breakfast without you." Pulling me into his chest, I breathed him in and instantly calmed. He had that power over me. All my fears melted when he was close. "How are you feeling? You look a little pale, Straight Lace."

"I'm fine. Don't fuss." He had enough going on; he shouldn't have to worry about my small freak out last night.

"It's my job to fuss." Alex frowned at me. "Something is wrong. I can tell by your face." I couldn't keep anything from him. "Come on, out with it!"

I had to think of something fast. I couldn't tell him the truth. It might jeopardize the whole tour. "David tried to make a pass at me last night." I winced the moment the words came out of my mouth. How was that any better than the truth?

"He fucking what?!"

"I handled it though!"

"That doesn't fucking matter. That fucker shouldn't be going anywhere near you!" Alex took a few deep breaths to calm himself, but it didn't look like it was working. "I need to sort that fucker out once and for all. He's been pushing his fucking luck since the moment he joined Rock Records!"

"That's exactly what he wants—knowing that he's getting

to us." Alex looked ready to kill David. I couldn't allow that.

"But he *is* getting to us. I can see it in your eyes, Straight Lace." My eyes began to water as he touched my face. It was dangerous that Alex knew me so well. "I don't ever want to make your eyes water, Baby. That's not the life I want for us."

"Can we just change the subject? I'm really hungry." Alex started to shake his head but then agreed with a nod before leading me into the breakfast room.

"Have you read the reviews from last night's show?" Cody was jumping up and down like an excited kid as he got onto the tour bus. The logistics behind this world tour were crazy—one hundred and twenty trucks had gone ahead of us to move the stage, screens, lights, and two hundred and fifty speakers to the next venue, which happened to be Modena in Italy. Unlike Rome, we were doing two nights there.

"At least the write up wasn't all about Alex for once," Matt sneered from the back of the coach.

"I thought we'd talked about this. The band isn't just one person, Matt. I'm so fucking over this jealousy. Yes, I had a solo career. Get the fuck over it!" Alex looked worn out. I knew these conversations were more frequent these days. The relationship between him and Matt didn't seem to be getting any better.

"You left us all behind!" Matt spat.

"That's not really true," Mason piped up, trying to calm the situation down. "You've hated Alex for so long, it's ruling your judgement. Have you heard the crowds? They call for Steel Roses, not Alex. He's made sure of that. Not once has he tried to steal the limelight on this tour."

"You're defending him?" Disbelief was laced in Matt's

voice.

"Someone has to!" Mason looked over towards Alex. "He's been fighting these battles alone. Cody and I have had enough of your bullshit, Matt. Get the fuck over it, or we'll replace you! We're not letting you ruin this tour!"

"Replace me?!" Matt roared. "You're all in on this?! Alex has corrupted your minds! This band is *nothing* without me!"

"Get over yourself, Asshole" Cody chuckled. "You're just the guitar player with a massive chip on his shoulder. You are the only one bringing this tour down."

"Is that how you all feel?" Matt looked around at his bandmates. None of them spoke. In one swift motion, Matt was out of the tour bus and storming back into the hotel.

"Shouldn't we go after him?" Alex muttered, shock was all over his beautiful face.

"Fuck him." Cody looked towards the driver. "Let's go."

Had Matt just left the band after the first night?!

CHAPTER TEN

Matt didn't return like most of us thought he would. The hatred clearly ran too deep with him and Alex. We had no idea if he'd be back to finish the tour. Luckily, Alex called in a few favors and found an amazing guitarist called Max to stand in while we waited for Matt to make his decision. The band's chemistry on stage with Max was electric. As sad as I felt for Matt, the fans didn't seem to miss him too much either.

We were three months into the tour and currently back in Italy. I'd lost count of the number of cities we'd visited in Europe. The logistics weren't that easy with venues, so there was a lot of back and forth. When Alex and I had discussed the tour back in LA, I had imagined seeing the world. In reality, all we saw were hotel rooms. The cities flew by in a blur from the tour bus.

"Can you believe the tour is a quarter way through?" Liv sighed while we were soaking up the sunshine on our private rooftop in Milan. "I feel like it's going too fast."

"We'll be on the US leg of the tour before we know it."

"Alex seems a lot calmer, too."

"Matt walking out bonded the rest of the band. Alex never thought they would choose him over Matt. It's made him realize how much he's changed. He's enjoying this tour more than he ever thought he would."

"You've grounded him, Natty. Shane and I have taken bets when he'll propose to you." My mouth dropped open as I listened to her. Where had this conversation suddenly come from? "Oh, come on! You must have thought about it. The guy is head over heels in love with you."

"I can't *marry* Alex," I gasped. "He'll tire of me before we get to that point."

"You don't see yourself very clearly. Diego thinks you have insecurity issues and I'm starting to agree with him."

"Don't you have better things to do that talk about me?"

"Ummmm... No, not really," Liv giggled. It was a good job she was my oldest and dearest friend. "What if he's already asked your dad if he can marry you, and he's just waiting for the right time?"

"Can we change the damn subject?! This is meant to be relaxing." I had enough on my mind without thinking about marriage to a rock star!

"Would you say yes if he asked?"

"LIV!" I yelled. "Shut the fuck up!"

"Okay, moody," Liv teased. "I think you'd say yes, anyway." I closed my eyes, not responding to her answer. I didn't think Alex was the marrying type.

I must have fallen asleep, because the next thing I felt was Diego shaking me awake. "Wake up, Cupcake. We have shopping to do."

"Shopping?" I groaned, stretching. "I don't need anything."

"You've forgotten about the fashion awards tonight, haven't you?" Crap, that was tonight? "For a PA, you're awful at organizing your own calendar. Oh, wait, Liv is meant to do that for you." I snorted at the bitch brow Liv was giving Diego. "The car is waiting. You two need to get changed quickly."

I'd never seen price tags for clothes like the ones in Milan. How could a piece of material cost so much? Diego, of course, was in his element. He'd even found a bowtie for Ralph for when he flew back to him in a few days. He was the best dressed dog in the world. Diego never left it more than ten days without flying back to him. It wasn't like he needed to be here for all of the world tour, anyway.

"What about this? Your skin tone is perfect to pull it off." Diego was holding a shimmering, long, silver silk dress.

"I don't know, I was thinking black might…"

"Bitch, no one has died! You don't *need* to wear black. At least try this on. Fashion is my job, after all." Diego batted his perfect eyelashes at me. Snatching the dress off him, I went into the changing rooms.

The man was right, of course. I looked like a goddess in the dress, but I wasn't looking to draw any attention to myself tonight. "Can I try the black dress on please?" I called from the dressing room.

"Nope, not until you come out in that one." I rolled my eyes before finally stepping out so Diego could see me. "Damn, girl! That's the one! You don't need to try the black dress!" He had a look on his face that told me I wasn't going to win this argument.

"Whatever happened to freedom of choice?" I complained. "I know you're a fashion advisor, but at times you are so fucking *annoying*."

"Now you sound like Alex," Diego grinned. "He's clearly rubbing off on you in more ways than one." I knew he was being dirty but I wasn't going to rise to it. Jeez, even my inner thoughts were dirty. Maybe Alex *was* rubbing off on me too much.

"Okay, I'll buy the damn dress!" Diego had a victory smile on his face as I walked over to pay for it.

"Who are we likely to see tonight?" Liv asked as we made our way back to the hotel. "Can I bring my autograph pad?" I had to giggle. She'd had that pad since we were kids and had only recently started getting decent celebrities to sign it. Alex and the rest of the band had signed the front page, of course. They were her childhood, just like they'd been mine.

"If you can fit it in that tiny purse you're taking out, yes, but do *not* walk around with it in your hand! I will not be seen dead with you if you're hunting for autographs," Diego teased. "You can be such an embarrassment at times." Liv slapped him playfully. "You've got your slutty dress ready for tonight, right?"

"Of course," Liv grinned. Diego was becoming a bad influence on her.

It didn't matter how many red carpet events I'd been to, they still made me feel uneasy. Perhaps it was because I felt as if I didn't fit in. I'd always been a behind the scenes type of person. This was Alex's lifestyle, not mine.

"You look beautiful, Straight Lace," Alex whispered in my ear. "You're going to make it difficult to keep my eyes off you tonight." I tried to hide my blush. He really could be the sweetest man when he spoke to me like that.

"I'm sure your fans will keep you busy enough," I teased, pointing over to the crowd of females that were all screaming his name. "Go do your job, Rock Star. I'll be here waiting for you." Cody and Masen were already making their way over to the fans, but the yelling got louder as Alex approached them.

"Shall we get the drinks in, ladies?" Diego asked Liv and I. "The boys might be a while with that lot." Liv and I nodded and followed him into the large function room.

"Oh fuck! Hold me back! I could get so many autographs in here!" Liv was like an over excited puppy. "Is that a member of our royal family?!" She gasped for air.

"I've got to go and check Alex's timings for the award he's giving." I turned towards Diego. "You'll have to go with her and make sure she doesn't make a fool of herself."

"That ship sailed long ago, Baby Cakes." Diego rolled his eyes but still followed Liv as she darted into the crowd of people.

I managed to find the events team and get the timings for Alex. Luckily, he was giving out one of the earlier awards so we wouldn't be here all night. I'd already written out his little speech with the help of Diego, so he was good to go.

I bumped into a few familiar faces as I searched the crowd for Alex. It felt strange that people noticed me because I was his PA and had been pictured with him a few times in the media.

My eyes finally found him, surrounded by females as I expected, but suddenly I froze. What the fuck was Madison Lily doing standing with her fake blonde hair extensions, laughing at everything he said?

I tried to compose myself with everything that I could, but images of her and Alex kept flashing through my mind. He'd dipped his dick in that whore and I couldn't shake the thought from my mind!

Alex's eyes suddenly caught mine, panic was written all over his face. I shook my head, unable to meet his gaze anymore. I couldn't do this. I couldn't walk over to that group of women all lusting after Alex, knowing Madison was there. He shouldn't keep putting me in these situations! It wasn't fair!

Fighting the tears, I turned around and tried to escape, but Alex gently grabbed my arm before I could move too far. "Nat, wait! What could I do? She was with a group of her friends."

"I don't know, but we can't do this here! People are looking!"

"Do you think I give a fuck if people are looking? You're upset. I'm not letting you leave like this."

"I can't do this here, Alex, please."

"You can't do what?" I was about to answer, but of course Madison had to come over and interrupt.

"Natasha, I thought that was you! What's Alex's schedule like this week? I'd love some *quality* time with him." Resisting the urge to scratch her eyes out, I took a deep breath to regain my calm.

"I'm pretty busy with the tour, Madison." Alex butted in, trying to pull me away. "Nice to see you, but Nat and I have things to discuss." *That was his response to her?!* He wasn't declining her offer, and he was being fucking nice to her!

"Actually, Alex is pretty free all week," I seethed, pulling out of his grip. "I'll let you two arrange all the sordid details. I'd love to say it's nice to see you, Madison, but I can't fucking stand you! Please don't ever speak to me again. Now, if you'll both excuse me!" My glare towards Alex told him not to follow me. I'd had enough tonight!

I was lucky that the event was so busy. It was easy to lose myself in the crowd. If Alex had tried to follow me he would have struggled.

Once I made it outside, I took a deep breath. What had

even just happened? I'd seen Alex with countless women over the last few months and kept my cool. Why had seeing him with Madison make me react that way? It wasn't even like she was an ex of Alex's, it had just been a fling. Knowing that didn't stop the anger surging through my body at the thought of them together, though. I'd always been a firm believer that your past was just that for a reason. There was no need to hold onto it and talk to it when it showed up!

"Nat?" a voice I vaguely recognized called from behind me. "I thought that was you." I groaned internally at seeing Lola, Matt's sister, standing in front of me. Was I going to end up seeing every one of Alex's conquests tonight? "I know Matt is being a dick at the moment, leaving the tour the way he did, but I don't want that to come between me and the band. Alex will always hold a special place in my heart." *Ugh!* Was everyone in love with Alex today?

"Lola, it's nice to see you. I'm just Alex's PA, I don't really have much control over the *band.*"

"Oh, that's not true. Everyone can see how much Alex looks for your input. You're more than his PA. He takes guidance from you."

"Have you heard from Matt?" Trying to steer the conversation from Alex and I seemed like a good idea. "The rest of the guys are worried about him."

"I seriously doubt that. They all hate my brother." Lola ran her hands through her shiny, perfectly cut blonde hair. "He's at a friend's house trying to work through his issues."

"Which friend?"

"I don't know, he didn't say. He's alive though. I'm sure he'll be in touch. He was pretty pissed that he got replaced by that Max guy."

"Max is just standing in. Matt walked out at the start of the world tour! What were they meant to do?"

"They could have gone after him. I know Matt is his own worst enemy at times, but he's pretty messed up. He's always felt like the outsider in the band."

"That's not the band's fault or Alex's, though." I was still angry with Alex, but I would stand up for him always. "Matt has been holding this grudge for too long. It's all in the past. He needs to let it the fuck go or it will destroy him."

"You know the whole story, don't you?"

"Yes, Alex confides in me." Lola quirked an eyebrow at me. "Do you have something else you want to say?"

"Has he got to you too? Is that why you're still hanging around? Do you honestly think *you* could get *Alex Harbour* to fall for you?" She laughed hysterically. This really wasn't my night. Lola was about to lose her teeth if she carried on. "Oh.My.God! You do think that! You poor, poor girl. Stop living in that little dream world of yours. You'll always just be the hired help, while women like *me* get the rock star." It appeared Lola was just as seething as her sibling. "You think you have a special bond with him, but you don't.. Are you fucking him? He usually likes a regular groupie to fuck on tour. He's just using you, you know. It's not going to go anywhere."

"Wow, I think someone has issues like her brother. What is it with your family, Lola? Are you all born a bit psychotic?" I snorted, shaking my head at her. "One moment you're telling me how Alex looks up to me, and now you think I'm doing all this for his affection! I'll let you in on a little secret. I fucking *hate* the man. He's a total man whore! If *your* type of woman wants him, then fucking be my guest. I want to make my life with someone who is capable of love, and that definitely isn't Alex Harbour!" Some of my words were true. At that moment in time I did hate him, but love was something I knew Alex was capable of.

It felt so good being able to direct my anger at someone. I almost felt sorry for Lola as she stood there gawking at me, unable to reply. "You need to get over yourself, Lola. Yes, your brother is in a famous rock band, but what have you ever done for yourself? You feed off Matt's fame and that is pretty pathetic."

"Well, you are just downright rude!" *That was all she could come up with?* "I'm going to make a complaint to Alex about you!"

"Be my fucking guest, you hypocritical bitch! What, you're allowed to be rude to me, but you can't handle it when it's given back?"

"I'm not standing here and taking this from you!"

"Alex is inside. Go…run to him. Once you're done with him, go tell your brother and how mean I've been. Oh, and while you're there, tell him to stop being a little pussy bitch and come back to the band if he's done moping around!" I'm not sure how I managed to swivel in my four inch heels, but I did, and strutted off just like Diego had taught me.

I didn't go straight back to the hotel. I had a feeling that Alex would already be waiting for me, and I wasn't ready for another argument yet. Milan was warm and still buzzing with life. I found a small coffee shop and sat in the corner, nursing a cappuccino. I must have looked a little out of place in the dress, because one of the waitresses asked if I was okay.

"I'm just having a bad night. I'm not quite ready to go

home and face the music." I smiled sadly.

"When you need a taxi, let me know and I'll call one." It was very sweet of her to offer, but I knew I'd be able to call Shane to get a lift. I hadn't even checked my phone, knowing I'd have lots of missed calls and messages. I'm not sure how long I sat looking at my cold cup of coffee, but when the waitress said she was closing soon, I had no choice but to call Shane.

He answered on the first ring. "Nat, where the fuck are you? Alex is going crazy with worry!"

"Is he there?"

"No, he's in the other room about to sort out a search party for you! He thinks you've left him! What the hell happened earlier with Madison and Lola?" Fuck, Lola must have told Alex about our confrontation.

"Just come and get me. I'll deal with Alex when I'm ready." I gave Shane the address then hung up.

Alex standing on the pavement shouldn't have surprised me as I walked out of the coffee shop to meet Shane fifteen minutes later.

"You called Shane instead of me?" He sounded so pained as he spoke.

"I wasn't ready to talk to you." I pushed past him as Shane opened the car door for us. "I'm still not!"

"Fuck, Nat, what did I do? Why are you being like this?" I didn't even know how to answer that. I was being a bitch to him —I knew that—but I was hurting. I'd been in pain for months and it had finally all bubbled to the surface. I couldn't stop myself. "Baby, please, you're scaring me. Lola told me what you said. You think I'm a man whore, honestly?" Alex took my hand in his as he slid into the seat next to me. Trust Lola to tell him that part. "Talk to me. Whatever it is, we can sort it out."

"I'm angry with you!"

"You're stating the fucking obvious! Look, if this is about Maddison, the bitch came over to me with a group of her friends. What was I meant to do?"

"You could have thought about me! How did you think that would affect me? You have a history with Madison that *involves* me."

"What was I meant to do then? How the fuck would you have handled it?" I hated it when Alex turned it around on me. I wasn't sure how I'd have handled it. I probably would have grabbed Madison by her fake hair extensions and dragged her out of the event by her heels, but that would have drawn too much attention. "Well, I'm waiting! You're so fucking pissed at me, you must have an idea on what I should have fucking done?!"

"I shouldn't need to explain myself! You should have thought about me!"

"All I fucking do is think about you, Straight Lace. I *have* to talk to women. It's my fucking job! They are my main fanbase! Lola is just Lola. The girl has had the hots for me since she was a kid."

"I guess you should have kept your dick in your pants all those years ago. Then maybe she wouldn't be so obsessed with you!"

"Where is all this coming from? It's never bothered you before. This is all my past!"

"Why can't you just think about me. The first night of the tour you left me. You didn't even come to find me after the show. You were too caught up in all the stardom!"

"You never said..."

"You were on a high—I didn't want to bring you down."

"What...I have to second guess you, now? You said you weren't feeling well that night. You're so unpredictable. I have no fucking clue what I'm doing half the time on this fucking tour. I'm just following what Rock Records require of me! I can't stop talking to people of the opposite sex."

"You still don't get it!" It wasn't about *any* female! Alex could talk to whoever the hell he wanted, just not Maddison! Why couldn't he understand that? The bitch cheated on Shane with him. Alex had bedded her days after we took a break and that shit still hurt!

"Explain it to me then! What the fuck did I do?"

"You as good as cheated on me with Maddison! Does that make sense to you?"

"We were on a break! How can you think I cheated? I thought you didn't want me. How else was I meant to cope with how *I* was feeling?"

I sighed, defeated. I wasn't going to get him to understand that seeing him in bed with Maddison sliced me in two that night—that every time I saw them together, flashbacks would appear in my head and haunt me. He was turning this all back to how he had felt. "It just hurt me. Can you at least understand that?"

"Of course I fucking understand that! Fuck, Straight Lace, I warned you about this tour! I told you it wouldn't be easy. This *icon* I have to be for the fans, I fucking *hate* him. Do you think I *want* to be around all those bimbos? It's my fucking job to look like a ladies man. Rock Records write it into the contracts all the time. I know I've changed—I'm not that man anymore—yet for the sake of this fucking tour I have to revert back to a version of myself that repulses me. I don't even want to *go* to these media events, let alone talk to people. The only thing that keeps me going is seeing your face at the side of the stage. You're my lifeline. You're all that matters."

"I know that," I whispered, touching his face. His words had moved me.

"When this tour finishes I want us to go public. Then I can finally fucking breathe. If it's going to cause arguments all the time, I'm fucking done with this shit. " That was the first I'd heard of going public. Instantly, our fight was over. I had other things to panic about.

"That soon?" I gasped. There were only six months left of the tour. Was I ready to be thrown into the limelight as Alex Harbours girlfriend? Alex did have a point though; life would be easier once everyone knew we were together.

"It's not that soon." He smirked that dreamy smile that made my insides melt. I could never stay angry with *that* face. "We've been dating over a year now."

"Yeah, but it's a big step." Alex could hear the worry in my voice and wrapped his arm around me, pulling me closer towards him.

"You're it for me, Nat. I don't want to hide what I feel for you any longer than I have to." The car pulled up to the back of the hotel. Shane checked for press and groupies before we got out and made our way inside through the kitchen. It amazed me how many back doors we'd had to sneak through to hide from people on this tour.

Alex and I were quiet as we made our way up to the penthouse suite. I could feel the electricity surging between us, though, as we reached the lift.

I was scared to look at him. The desire seeping through my veins was too strong. What was it about Alex and I in confined spaces?

"You know what I want to do to you, right?" Sex dripped from Alex's voice as he spoke.

Clenching my legs together, I tried to answer him. "N...No, what do you want to do?"

"I want to fuck you until your body can't take anymore." Swallowing hard, I slowly looked up at him. "I'm going to tease you for hours. Your body is going to beg for my cock, but I won't let you have it until I'm ready." I was sure if you could cum from words alone, I would have in that moment.

Alex kept his distance until the elevator doors opened, but his hungry stare made it impossible for me to move a single inch.

"Run, Straight Lace." Alex motioned towards the open doors with a devilish grin on his face. My legs were trembling so much that he caught me within seconds as I tried to make my escape in my heels. "You made that too easy for me," he whispered into my ear, biting down on my earlobe.

"Maybe I wanted to make it easy for you." I could hardly recognize my own voice. I was so turned on I sounded like a porn actress.

"Oh, you're giving in that easily?" He pushed me against the wall with his own body. I could feel his bulge against my ass as he ran his hands down my side. "Shall I play with you here in public? I'm so glad you're wearing a dress tonight." Fuck! I'd forgotten we weren't even in the penthouse yet.

Alex's hand moved towards my behind. He gripped my

butt firmly, moving his fingers between my cheeks so he could get to my sex. I let out a gasp as he ran his fingers over my clit through my panties.

"Oh Baby, I can feel how wet you are already. This is going to be so much fun." Bracing myself against the wall, I tried to regulate my breathing in time with each stroke of his fingers. It was a torturous pleasure. Alex's pace was so slow, and every time I felt myself build he stopped. He hadn't even placed his fingers under my panties yet and I was burning to feel them inside me.

"Let's take this inside so I can slowly undress you." I could hear the desire deep in his voice as he released his hold on me.

"I can hardly stand."

"Oh, if you think that now…wait until later." He winked, moving to the penthouse door.

I knew once I stepped through the door I was going to be in trouble. It was funny how I practically skipped into the penthouse lobby even in four inch heels.

CHAPTER ELEVEN

The moment Alex shut the penthouse door, he was on me. His hands were greedy and I felt him everywhere at once.

He was quick to remove my dress so I was standing before him in just my red lace panties and bra.

"Fuck, Straight Lace! You are so fucking sexy. You know that, right?"

"Don't stop touching me," I begged when he took a step back to admire me.

"Are you begging already?" he teased, moving closer towards me to stroke my legs. "I've hardly started."

"Please touch me. You're driving me crazy!"

"That's the idea. Where do you need me to touch you?" *He fucking knew where I wanted his fingers!* "I'm not a mind reader. You need to tell me."

"You *know* where I want your fingers!" I pleaded.

"Your breasts?" He gripped both my breasts firmly before slipping one hand inside my bra to tease my right nipple. "Was this what you wanted?" In between my legs was beginning to burn. Any more of this glorious torture and I was sure I'd pass out. "No? What about this?" His fingertips moved down to my stomach. My hips bucked up towards him, trying to urge his fingers to where I needed them the most but they detoured. I let out a gasp of frustration as he caressed my thighs. They were so close to the sweet spot that I wanted so desperately for him to explore.

"Am I driving you crazy enough, yet?" He grinned as he inched his hand closer towards my sex.

"ALEX!" I yelled. "Take my fucking panties off now before I fucking combust!!" I was done begging; that was a fucking demand!

"Oh, was that an order?"

"If you ever want me to agree to go public with our relationship...yes!!" I was starting to sound desperate, but I needed him to touch me right now!

"Oh, you're playing that game," he chuckled, moving his hands to slowly pull my panties down my legs. It was still not fucking fast enough. Once my panties hit the floor, I kicked them off my one ankle. Alex roughly forced my legs further apart and lifted me so I was sitting on the table. "You'll need to sit for this," he whispered, moving in to kiss my lips. The moment our mouths touched, I felt his fingertips against my clit. Jolts of electricity seemed to surge around my body as he began to gently rub my sex. I grabbed his shoulders tightly, trying to ground myself. I knew that when I finally climaxed, I was going to lose control completely.

His other hand moved to unhook the clasp on my bra. The moment my breasts were free, his lips moved from my mouth to my left breast. His tongue rolled around my nipple before he teased it with his teeth. With his fingertips starting a faster pace on my sex, I knew I didn't have long until I fell.

My whole body began to tremble as the climax started to build.

"That's it, Straight Lace, give it up. Then I can carry you to our bed and slam my cock inside you!" At his words I came undone, moaning out as I climaxed. *Holy fuck! That was an orgasm!*

Alex was true to his word—before I'd even come down from my pure pleasure ride, I felt my body hit the mattress softly.

"I hope you're ready for this. I want to hold off your orgasm for as long as possible. You're going to feel so sore in the morning." Why did I love that thought so much?!

The moment I felt him slide inside me I began to yearn for more of him. My body was made for this—for his pleasure and mine. It would always belong to him. Noone ever made it sing the way Alex did. Nothing had ever even come close.

In that second I realized nothing would ever compare for either of us. This was it for *both* of us. Whatever came our way, we'd get through it...together. This was more than love. This was soul crushing, heart devouring, and body consuming need for one another.

By the time Alex finally let me climax, we came as one. I lay there listening to him trying to catch his breath, the same as me.

It was still difficult to wrap my head around my feelings for him. This was more than I'd ever dreamed of. I had always dreamed about being so in love, but to have the strength of that love returned was the best feeling in the world. Add to that the fact that it was Alex Harbour that loved me! Why had I been fighting going public? Why did I need to be afraid that everyone would know once the world tour ended? Alex was my forever. I didn't have to worry anymore.

"How sore are you?" Alex mused, moving to wrap his arms around me.

"Very, but it's good sore," I grinned. "I'm glowing in all the right places."

"Glowing?"

"It's the only way I can describe it," I giggled. "I'm sorry I was a bitch earlier."

"I love you, Straight Lace. You have nothing to fear. I'm going nowhere. I'm yours."

"I know." I touched his beautiful face before leaning up to kiss his lips softly. "I'm yours, too. I love you so much. Once the tour finishes, I want to go public. I'm ready."

"You are?!" His eyes widened in surprise. "What changed your mind?"

"Apart from the out of this world orgasm? I don't want to hide this anymore."

"Well, if it's orgasms that help me get my way, maybe we need a few more." I giggled as he moved on top of me. The second his lips touched mine, I was lost again.

Liv and I sat watching Alex rehearse while we drank our coffee. We were now in Germany—Munich, to be precise—in one of their large, outdoor stadiums. The European portion of the tour was almost over. I would never tire of listening to Alex when he did an unplugged session by himself as practice. There was something magical about his voice and a single guitar.

"You seem calmer this week." Liv was looking at me suspiciously. "Did you and Alex have a fight and then make up?"

"What makes you think that?"

"Diego said you two have been acting like horny teenagers

every time he walks into the penthouse."

"Diego needs to learn to knock before he enters a room. Otherwise, Alex will take away his access to the penthouse," I chuckled, thinking back to the few times Diego had walked in on Alex and me in the last week. He was right, though. Alex and I had been acting like we'd only just got together. We were so much more relaxed in our relationship now that we'd decided when to go public. Strangely, I wasn't afraid anymore. I wasn't doing this to prove a point to anyone. I was just *finally* being honest with everyone about the man that I was in love with.

Liv was about to say something until Diego rushed in and caught our attention. He waved at Alex, motioning him to stop playing.

Liv and I had reached the stage by the time Diego began to talk. "You will never believe who has finally come back with his tail between his legs!"

"Matt?" Alex was as shocked as us. "Is he here?"

"He's in the green room. He wants to talk to you alone. He reeks of bourbon, though." I got the impression that Diego didn't think it was a good idea for Matt and Alex to speak privately.

"Your chat with Lola must have worked," Alex smirked, looking at me. Holy Shit. Was this because of me? "Right, let's get this shit done. Then we can carry on with this fucking tour!"

"You're going to talk to him alone?" Diego gasped. "Are you completely *insane*?"

"Diego, you don't need to fight my battles for me. I'm a big boy now."

"But Matt is a complete *moron*! You'll never make him see sense."

"It's not about making him see sense. It's about him

having his say so he can heal. He never got over Ness and needs closure. I owe him that much. He's part of Steel Roses. He deserves this tour as much as the rest of us." We were all looking at him in awe. When did Alex become so wise?

"Go and talk to him then." Alex didn't need reassurance from me, but I wanted him to know that I was behind him. He nodded, then jumped off the stage in the search of Matt.

Hours had passed and we were all pacing in the canteen area that had been set up for the band and crew.

It was difficult to not act as concerned as I really was. To most of the people in this room, I was just Alex's PA.

"Shane, I really think you need to go and check on them. We heard some raised voices a while ago. What if they're in there trying to kill each other?" Cody was on edge like the rest of us.

"I didn't hear anything being broken. Let's just give them a bit more time. They have a lot to talk through." Shane did have a point, but my primary concern was and always would be Alex.

"Alex would win the fight anyway," Diego chuckled. "When has Matt ever won anything in the years they've known each other?"

"Do you remember the cock battle tour?" Mason snorted. "Matt tried that dick enlarger, but still had the smallest cock."

"I think we all knew who had the smallest cock from the start," Naomi, the tour manager snorted. She'd been alerted to Matt's return by one of the crew. "But I'll never forget him getting it stuck in that thing."

"He couldn't look us in the eye for days." Cody laughed.

"Matt's always been a weird fucker," Naomi commented. "I can't believe he's come back, though. His pride is too strong for that shit usually."

"And you wonder where he got his issues from? Everyone has always been against him. I've told you all this before—he's a lot more sensitive than you think." Gina suddenly appeared out of nowhere. She had a habit of doing that. "Where are they?" We all pointed to the green room. "Right, it's time to bash their heads together. I'm done with this crap!" She stormed into the room without hesitation, and I could only hope that Alex and Matt were ready for the wrath of Gina.

Another hour went by before Alex and Matt finally emerged from the green room. They looked like naughty school boys that had been told off by the headmistress .

"Guys, I know I've been a total jerk." Matt didn't even look up as he spoke. "I'm sorry. I really want to finish this tour with you guys. I've apologized to Alex. I'm not going to hold a grudge anymore. Can we start afresh?" Of course Cody and Masen welcomed him back. I wasn't sure how sincere Matt was being, but we only had six months left anyway. What damage could he do in that time? Alex gave me a little wink over his shoulder while the band had a group hug, assuring me that everything was okay. I couldn't wait to find out what had gone on in that room, though.

I'd been pleading for an hour for Alex to fill me in on all the details. "So you just had it out and everything was cool?" I frowned.

"Yes, I keep telling you, Matt is a changed guy. He had a go at me for Ness, but then said we'd put it in the past. I have no idea what soul searching he's done, but he's finally moved on."

"What did Gina say?"

"She made Matt promise to not bring anymore shit up. Otherwise he's out of the band for good." *Wow! Go Gina!* "It's all done and dusted, Straight Lace. You can stop worrying about me." Alex kissed my forehead lovingly.

"But that's my job as your girlfriend," I giggled. "I'll never trust him, but if you're cool with this then so am I."

"We've got four more shows in Europe, then we're on the final leg back home. Let's just enjoy this so you and Liv get the best groupie experience possible." He thought he was so funny at times. Two could play at that game.

"This *is* quite the experience," I murmured, running my hands down his chest. "I mean, I get to fuck the front man of the band."

"Oh baby, you can have him *anytime* you want him." His words sent chills down to my core.

"Mmmm...in that case, I think I'll have him right now," I whispered, climbing on top of Alex. I'd never get bored of this kind of power.

"Don't break the line!" Shane yelled at his team as they tried to control the crowd. Word had gotten out that Steel Roses was having some down time in a VIP nightclub, and now the place was rammed with groupies. It didn't matter which country we were in, there was always a whistleblower, but France seemed *extra* crazy. "Archie, don't let them fucking through! We need to keep this exit clear!" I hadn't seen Shane this irate in a while. Half of the band was safely through. It was just Matt, Mason, Diego and myself that were still trying to fight our way past the crowd. "I'm going to start head butting these fucking groupies in a minute! You guys go through there. I'll be back once I've sorted this crowd out!"

"They're our bread and butter, man! Don't be so harsh." Matt chuckled, turning to look at me. "Ladies first?" He gestured for me to go through the door before him. I still wasn't used to nice Matt. He'd only been back a few weeks, and to me it was like he was trying too hard.

"Thanks." I tried my best to smile at him sincerely. "Diego, come on bitch tits!" I called, not wanting Matt to be too close behind me.

"Queens coming through," Diego announced as we made our way into a secure room. "Fuck, there are some crazy ones out tonight. Once bitch pulled my hair."

"I bet you liked it, really," Alex chuckled.

"If it had been a hunky man maybe! I can't be doing with female foreplay. It's too scratchy, anyway. Not to mention moany."

"What's fucking wrong with scratchy?" Matt asked, pouring himself a glass of whiskey from the small bar in the corner of the room. "I like nail marks down my back. It means I've done my job fucking her right."

"When was the last time you got laid? The eighties?" Cody snorted. "And pour me a glass, too. If we're going to be stuck in here for a while, we might as well get drunk!"

Alex rubbed his neck. I could see the tension all over his face. These were the times he struggled with his alcoholism— when the rest of the band went on a bender. He couldn't even leave the room for a distraction.

"Front man, are you having one?" I wanted to smash the

bottle in Matt's face as he called over to Alex. "For old times' sake? It's your favorite bourbon."

"Why don't you offer him some crack, too, you fucking idiot!" Diego snapped. "What part of *he's a recovering addict* do you not understand?"

"He can speak for himself! I was just asking a friend if he wanted a drink."

"I'm good, thanks." Alex smiled as he moved to sit on one of the four red couches. "I might have a ginger beer, though, if there are any?" Matt found one and threw it over to him.

"How about a game while we wait for Shane and his team to disburse the crazy crowd?" Matt suggested, taking a seat. That was the best idea he'd ever had. "I'm thinking truth or dare!"

"We're not twelve," Mason snorted. "Don't we have a deck of cards or something? Nat, you're our PA. What have you got in your bag?"

"I don't have a deck of cards. I've got some throat sweets and some lip gloss."

"Truth or dare it is, then." Matt clapped his hands together in excitement. "I know most of you fuckers pretty well, but this could be fun!"

The game started off pretty tame. Most picked truths and we learnt about past conquests and random orgies from his early days in the band. Some were pretty funny, and it was nice seeing the guys all getting on. It was like I was getting a small snippet of what it had been like being for Steel Roses when they were at their peak.

"Fuck it! I'll have a dare. I'm sick of truths now!" Alex was still chuckling from the revelation that Cody had had sex with his mum's best friend.

"You sure?" Matt raised an eyebrow at him.

"Yes, motherfucker! Do your worst. We can't leave this room, so how bad could it be?"

"Kiss Nat." *Oh fuck!*

"What? She's my PA. I'm not doing that." How Alex remained so calm in these situations I never knew.

"You've fucked plenty of females you shouldn't have!" Cody slurred. "It's just a fucking kiss! Do it! Do it! Do it." Mason joined in on the chanting. Fuck, Alex and I were going to have to do this!

"Oh, if it will shut you fuckers up! Is it okay if I kiss you, Natalie?" Why was Alex's use of my full name so hot? I nodded nervously, licking my lips and swallowing hard as he stood up to make his way towards me.

"With tongues, too!" Mason cheered. He was the light weight of the band and totally drunk.

Alex held his hand out to help me stand. Gently, he placed one hand on my waist, pulling me towards his chest. I felt as if I was going to melt into his embrace. Tilting my head up towards his, Alex's lips gently pressed against mine. Now was the time to act like we'd never done this before. I gasped into his mouth, trying not to get too carried away as his fingers dug into my hips. His tongue slowly darted in to meet mine for a brief second before he pulled back.

"Damn, Nat, you can kiss!" he teased, moving back so I could sit down again. *Jesus! Why had that been so fucking hot?*

"Nat, you look a bit flustered there. Are you okay?" Matt questioned. Something in his stare made me uneasy.

"I'm fine. It's not every day you get to snog your boss," I tried to joke.

"At least you don't make a habit of it." Was there a hidden meaning in his reply or was I just being paranoid?

Diego took a turn next and soon the kiss was just a memory. Everyone was getting more daring as the night went on. Mason ended up having to lick Cody's nipple. Diego had to kiss Alex, which was pretty funny. He was shocked at how Alex really got into it.

"You taste like ham! What the fuck have you been eating?" Diego wiped his mouth in disgust. Alex was laughing so hard that he had to hold his stomach. "I honestly don't get what the groupies see in you."

"It's the cheek bones," Cody snorted. "And the massive cock, probably."

"I'm a good kisser, admit it!" Alex chuckled.

"I felt like I was kissing a blowfish."

Cody spun the bottle again and it landed on Matt. "Oh, I've got a good one. Kiss Nat. Maybe she could get around the whole band by the end of the night." Why did Cody have to come up with that?!

Alex went rigid, but then corrected himself. I was sure I was the only person to notice it.

"I'm up for that if Nat is!" Matt quirked an eyebrow, looking over at me.

"I think snogging me was enough for one night." Alex was trying his best to act unaffected, but I wasn't sure it was working. "Leave the poor woman alone."

"It's just a kiss. We aren't fucking her," Cody sniggered. "Go on, Nat!"

"Cupcake isn't going to kiss that mouth! We *all* know where it's been." It was sweet watching Diego and Alex try to protect me, but I couldn't see that I had any other choice.

"Why are you two protecting her?" Matt mused. "The poor girl might want a bit of fun. I have to admit, I've thought about my lips on her since the moment I saw her. You are sexy as fuck, Nat."

Everything happened so quickly in that instant. Diego practically jumped on Alex's back to stop him from charging towards Matt. Masen and Cody had no clue what was going on or what had caused Alex's rage.

"She is fucking off limits, Matt! Do you fucking understand that, motherfucker?!" Alex's tone was deadly.

"Oh, I think you've got the hots for your PA!" Matt let out a roar of laughter. "What, are you two trying to keep it professional but the sexual attraction is making it difficult?"

"Let's change the subject!" Diego was still holding on to Alex. "You've all had too much to drink. You know the fights break out when you're all like this. Things have been going well between you guys tonight—don't ruin it now."

"Alex is sober! What's his fucking excuse?" Matt yelled, laughing to himself.

"Nat means a lot to me as a *friend*. I'm not having her passed around like some fucking groupie!" He was about to snap; I could tell by the way he was looking at me.

Shane suddenly appeared, breaking all the tension. "Okay guys, it's all clear. We can leave out the back now. I've got three cars waiting to take us back to the hotel."

"Fucking finally!" Alex was the first to leave the room. "I've just about had enough of all this bullshit tonight." I didn't follow straight behind. I knew we'd get a chance to talk about tonight when we were back at the hotel. Just what was Matt playing at?

"Do you think Matt knows?" I asked Alex later that night once we got back.

"I honestly don't know. How the fuck could he have found out? It just makes no sense."

"It wasn't like it was his idea to kiss me. Maybe he just got lucky? Everyone was pretty drunk tonight."

"Hopefully, Straight Lace. I didn't like what the fucker said about you, though. If he so much as looks at you in the wrong way, I'll kill him!"

"He was drunk. I'm sure all this will be forgotten about tomorrow." I didn't believe my words, but I had to try and comfort Alex. I was beginning to suspect that Matt had come back to the band to cause more trouble.

"You're right. Now let's get back to that dare kiss. The way your lips trembled against mine made my dick stand at attention."

"I can't believe how fucking turned on I was! And trying to hide it was so exciting," I giggled. Alex looked down at me hungrily. I bit my lip, knowing that at any second, his mouth would claim mine. It was such a sweet surrender when he did, and I gave in gladly. We both needed the distraction after the night we'd had.

CHAPTER TWELVE

How do you keep yourself together while you watch the person you love more than anything lose his battle with his demons? It had been a few weeks since the truth and dare saga, and things had pretty much gone back to normal. Matt seemed to have forgotten most of that night, and nothing more was mentioned.

It was our last few days in Europe. Liv and I had decided to go back home to London for a long weekend to see our family and friends before the world tour did its final leg in the USA. It had been wonderful to see my parents and spend some quality time with them.

"Four days away from Shane and I miss him like crazy!" Liv sighed as the plane touched down in Zurich, Switzerland. Tonight was the last European show for Steel Roses. "Do you think he's missed me?"

"Liv, of course he has! It's only been four days, though." I looked down at my phone. I hadn't heard from Alex for over a day and was starting to worry. It was so unlike him.

"Have you still not heard from him?" Liv asked, concerned. "Do you think he's okay?"

"I'm not sure," I whispered. I needed to get the hotel Alex was staying at so I could ease my mind. "Diego hasn't replied to me, either."

"Maybe the signal is down here? Shane only sent me a quick message and then said he was really busy and couldn't talk." Something didn't add up, and my fear was that something bad had happened to Alex.

Why did things take so long when you were in a hurry? Even being in first class didn't seem to really speed up the airport. It was almost an hour later before Liv and I could get a taxi. Traffic was slow in Zurich as we glided through the city. It was late afternoon, and everyone seemed to be out and getting in our way. We drove past Hallenstadion, the stadium Steel Roses would be playing at tonight, then finally pulled up outside the hotel ten minutes later.

I raced into the lobby and quickly as I could. Diego was in reception waiting for me. One look on his face and my eyes began to tear up. This *was* to do with Alex.

"Where is he?" I begged, running over to him.

"Baby Cakes, you need to sit down. I need to explain to you what's happened before you see him."

"Is he okay?" Tears were trickling down my face, and I didn't care who saw them. Liv took a seat next to me and put her hand in mine.

"He's okay," Diego took a deep breath. "He's relapsed, but it wasn't his fault. Someone spiked his drink with ketamine on Friday and he ended up doing a few lines of coke because he was so out of it." *Fuck! No!* "But...he's got a taste for it again. He's been high all weekend and has been drinking, too. Gina wants him to go to rehab for two weeks, but he's not listening. All he cares about is his next hit." I felt as if my heart was collapsing in my chest with each word that Diego spoke.

"H…H…Has he asked for me?"

"Breathe, Nat." Liv soothed, squeezing my hand to let me know she was here for me.

"He breaks down each time I've mentioned you. I don't know if he'll want to see you. I have no idea if it'll make him worse."

"Why would I make him worse?" I had to see him. I was the only one that could save him. He'd been fighting his demons more easily because of *me*. Why couldn't Diego see that?

"He's ashamed, Baby Cakes. He doesn't want you to see him like this. He thinks he's failed you."

"No, I need to see him. Right now!" I wiped my eyes and stood up. "If he's ashamed, he can fucking see me and stop his next hit!" I had no idea where all this strength was coming from, but I wasn't going to let Alex go through this alone. I loved him, and as much as it terrified me to come face to face with his addiction, I wasn't going to give up on him. "Diego, I fucking mean it. Take me to him *now!*" Something in my voice must have scared him. Wordlessly, he got up and led me towards the lift.

"Shane is outside. I'm going to go find him," Liv called. "Ring me if you need me." I nodded in her direction but was hardly paying attention. My whole mind was on Alex and how I was going to cope with seeing him under the influence of coke and whatever else he'd been taking this weekend.

"Take a big breath," Diego whispered as we stood outside Alex's bedroom. "It's hard to see when you're not used to it. This is going to rip you in half." Diego was trying to hide his tears. I reached out and hugged him.

"I'll make him come back. I'm stronger than I look." I wish I believed my words, but I wanted to give Diego some hope. He loved Alex so much. They were family in so many ways.

"I'll be outside if you need me. If he gets...angry, keep your distance. He can be volatile and throw things." That didn't sound like Alex at all, but I guess that was the drugs and alcohol controlling him. "And remember, this isn't him."

"Okay, I'm ready." I wasn't, but I'd never move if I didn't make myself.

The suite was quiet as I walked in. I tried to listen to see if I could work out which room Alex was in. There were only three doors, so I didn't have many rooms to check. The first was the bathroom, and it was empty.

Moving to open the second room, I heard a glass smash and someone mutter to themselves. Alex was behind *that* door. I braced myself, not knowing what I was about to face, and pushed the door open.

My eyes fell on a stare that I thought I knew, but the more I studied his face, I realized I could have been looking at a total stranger. His eyes were dilated and red. They looked too alive and wired. How much had he taken this weekend?

"I told Diego *not* to let you in," Alex seethed. His cheeks were flushed, and his words were slurred. I was breaking piece by piece with every step I took towards him. "You can't be here!"

"Where else would I go, Alex?" I pleaded. "Don't send me away."

"I don't want *this* with you. I don't want you to see this part of me. Do you understand?"

"When you told me about your demons, I accepted them. I've made them my own and I'm not afraid of them. I'm strong enough to face them with you. Let me help you, please!"

"YOU'RE NOT FUCKING LISTENING TO ME!" Alex roared,

throwing a beer bottle that was next to him onto the floor. I jumped back as some of the glass shards bounced in front of me. If Alex wanted a fight, he was going to get one because I wasn't going anywhere.

"No! You're not listening to me! You can have your child tantrums all you want, but I'm not going anywhere until we've talked!" I yelled, glaring at him. "You said you never wanted to lose me! This is part of the deal! We're meant to be there for each other, through the good and the bad. Are you saying you're giving up on us? Because I'll leave right now if that's the case!"

We both stood motionless, staring at each other. I crossed my arms, trying to look more threatening.

"Of course I'm not giving up! I just wanted you to see me once I'd come down from my high!"

"That may have taken days judging by the state of you. What the fuck have you been taking?"

"Mostly coke. I wanted to wait until I was fucking sober, too! You can't see me like this. I can't fucking deal with it!" He sulked, slumping down on the couch.

"I'd say your point is moot because I've seen you drunk before! We need to fucking talk!"

"What the fuck do you want to talk about then, smart arse?" Alex picked up the whiskey bottle from the floor and took a swig. It took all my strength not to beg him to put the bottle down. He'd tasted alcohol for the first time in over a year. It was going to take more than me begging to make him realize he didn't need it anymore.

"Oh, I don't know! Maybe the fact that I went away for *one* weekend and come back to find you like *this!*" I moved towards him and shoved at his chest. Anger was the only way to get through to him.

"You think I meant to do this?" He pulled at his hair, glaring down at me with his cold eyes. "My drink was spiked with something. I didn't take the drugs intentionally!"

"Someone made you snort those lines of coke on Friday, then?" He looked at me, shocked that I knew. "Yes, Diego's told me everything. Is that the same for the drink? Did someone make you do that, too?" I motioned towards the whiskey bottle. "Because it sure looks like you're drinking *that* intentionally!"

"Don't start with that self-righteous bullshit! I'm a recovering addict! You should know the two coincide with each other!"

"You're going to start with the excuses straight away, then. Okay. Well, if you're not going to listen, what good can I do?"

"I never said I was easy to fix! Fuck, I probably will always be this way. Why do you think I pushed you away at the beginning? I was petrified that you'd see me this way and realize you'd made a huge mistake. I wouldn't love me like this, Nat! My mother didn't love my father because he was the same way. I can't let you fall out of love with me like that. I can't let my monster win." My Alex was in there somewhere. His eyes softened as he gently caressed my face. "I don't want to live my life in fear that if I slip, I'll lose you."

"Why would you fear that? I'm not going anywhere." I reached out, touching his chest. "You said I'd changed you. You told me I was *the* reason to fight. Is that not the case anymore?"

"You have a hold on me, Straight Lace, believe me, but *this* has controlled me for over twenty years. It's hard to fight when I think the battle is lost."

"Don't say that," I whispered. "Tomorrow is another day. If you *need* to finish that whiskey bottle, I won't judge you, but once it's gone I want you to come back to me. Do you understand? You've got to fight this, Alex." Tears formed in his eyes. I caressed his beautiful, tormented face. "I'll be right here no matter how long the fight takes. I love every single part of you, even this excruciatingly tortured part. You'll never have to face this alone again. I promise." Alex's lips were hard against mine. He tasted of smoke and whiskey. I gasped into his mouth, shocked by the sudden advance. One second he'd been shouting, now his lips were pressed passionately against mine.

"Don't ever leave me, Nat," Alex pleaded against my lips. His hold on me felt as if I was the only thing keeping him grounded. "I don't think I could survive. You're the one thing I can't ever afford to lose. I'm sorry I've let you down."

"You haven't. You're human, Alex. You fight this every single day of your life. Don't be so hard on yourself."

"Can you take all the bottles away? I don't want to get distracted by them?"

"If you're sure?" When Alex nodded, I swiftly removed the few bottles left in the room and checked the rest of the hotel suite.

Diego was still outside as I opened the door. "How the fuck did you pry these off him?" he questioned in shock as I handed the bottles to him.

"He told me to remove them. You don't have to wait outside anymore. He's okay right now. I'll keep an eye on him tonight. Just give us some space. Can you let everyone else know? I'm guessing tonight's performance has been cancelled?"

"Yeah, Gina has done the press release and started issuing

the refunds. Unfortunately, they can't add it to another date either. The logistics don't work. If you need anything, call me." I hugged Diego tightly. "If anyone can get him back, I know it's you, Baby Cakes." Why didn't I have Diego's faith in myself?

"I'll let you know how he is in the morning," I called as Diego walked off.

Alex was lying on the couch when I re-entered the room. "The ceiling is spinning so much." He chuckled to himself. "I always used to like this out of control feeling. I'm not sure if it's the drugs or drink this time, though."

"What have you taken today?"

"Nothing too heavy...mostly some ketamine. I did a few lines of coke last night. That was all Matt had on hand."

"Matt?" I questioned. It was funny how his name kept coming up! "Why would he do that?"

"It's a habit, Nat. We used to get high every night in our earlier years. Matt's just as much of an addict as me. In fact, he's worse as he's never stopped using."

"Do you need anything? Water? Coffee? Chocolate?"

"It's not that easy coming down, Straight Lace," he snorted. "I wish it was as easy as just drinking some coffee."

"It might help the room to stop spinning."

"Just come and lie on the couch with me." He patted the space next to him. "I need a distraction." I quirked an eyebrow at him. He surely wasn't meaning sex while he was in this state? "I mean talking. Don't give me that look." Oh...now I was blushing. I snuggled in next to him and rested my head against his chest. "It's amazing how just the sound of your breathing is calming me. I never thought someone could hold that kind of power over me."

"Does that scare you?"

"It should, but it doesn't. It's control, but from a pure source. If I ever lost you, I know it would be from my own doing."

"Alex, you'd have to tell me to leave. I'm just as addicted to you. It would destroy me to lose you. You really don't need to fear losing me. How many times do I have to tell you that?" If I could give him peace of mind about us, at least I felt like I was helping his troubled mind in some way.

"I'll always fear that, Straight Lace. You'll always be too good for me." He kissed my forehead and I melted into him.

We must have fallen asleep for a few hours. Alex rolled over, almost squashing me. Somehow, I managed to slide off the couch without waking him up. I don't know how long I sat on the floor watching him sleep. He looked so peaceful. All the stress and despair had disappeared from his face. I wondered how he would feel when he awoke. Would he be hungover? Would he need another fix? Would he need something to eat? Maybe I needed to get some of his favorite chocolate? I was sure the hotel did twenty four hour room service. What if he woke up craving alcohol? Did I let him have it? I was such a novice at all this, but I had to take comfort in the fact that I knew Alex. I could figure out the rest as I went along.

It was becoming clear that Alex was a deep sleeper after taking a hit and drinking alcohol. He even snored like my dad. I had to chuckle to myself. Mum had always said I had to find a man like my dad. Alex did have a few of his qualities. He could sing a lot better than my dad, though.

Alex started muttering in his sleep. His words were nonsensical to begin with, but after a while it became clear what he was dreaming about.

"Ness, Ness...I'm sorry.... Matt will never forgive us. Ness, Ness...we can't do this anymore." Alex was dreaming about Vanessa. I don't know why it cut me in half so much. She was a past that Alex had long moved on from, but it was difficult to listen to him dreaming of her years after she'd passed away. Gazing down, I looked at the cross tattoo that was barely visible from his top. He'd marked himself for her. She had a permanent place near his heart. I didn't have that. "Matt, don't.... Matt, you can't end your life because of her." Alex was flinching in his sleep. Had Matt tried to take his own life after Vanessa? Alex had never mentioned that to me. "Why did she have to leave? I was just a kid! I *needed* her!" It felt wrong listening to his rambles, but I was mesmerized by this insight. "I...I can't explain it...sh...she completes me. I don't deserve her." Who was he talking about now? *Please, Alex, let this be about me!* "You don't understand! Let me explain." Was this about Vanessa? Didn't I feature in his dreams at all? "I *need* her! Don't ask me to give her up!" The more I listened, the more my heart sank. "No...come back! Please, don't do this! I need you!" Alex was reaching out in his sleep. His voice broke as he yelled. "Nat, please! Please don't leave. I'm sorry! Natasha!! Natasha!!" I had to wake him in that instant for both of our sakes. We were both breaking.

"Alex! Hey, it's okay! I'm here! I'm right here," I cooed, stroking his face. "It was just a nightmare." He finally opened his eyes.

"Fuck, I'd forgotten about my night terrors." Alex touched his forehead. "Fuck, I need some water. My head is throbbing." I wanted to offer him some painkillers but didn't think that would be a good idea.

"I'll get you some."

Alex was sitting up as I walked back into the lounge area. He was rubbing his face and pulling at his hair.

"Here." He took the glass of water and smiled up at me. It didn't reach his eyes, though. "Can you remember what you were dreaming about?"

"You left," he sighed. "I haven't had those since you walked out on me at the mansion." Alex had nightmares that one time I left him? I felt like a monster. "Fuck, I really need a drink!"

"What can I do?"

"Fuck me until I forget my own name?" I wasn't sure if Alex was teasing this time. "I'm being serious, Straight Lace." Fuck! Instantly, I was aroused. Was he letting me lead this time? I could take advantage of my rock star.

"Maybe we need to take this to the bedroom then?" I used the sexiest voice I could. It must have worked, because Alex practically ran to the bedroom. He was lying on the bed naked with his arms crossed behind his head when I walked in. *How fast did he get unchanged?*

"What are you going to do to me?"

"First, I need to get naked." I slowly took off each item of clothing. I'd never stripped for Alex before, but I felt so empowered watching his hungry stare.

"Fuck, Baby, hurry up and get over here!"

"All good things come to those who wait," I teased, standing before him in just my black lace underwear. I'd learnt to always wear lace these days. Crawling up the bed, Alex licked his lips, watching my cleavage until I was hovering above him. "Do I really get total control tonight?"

"Fuck yes. Just take me anyway you want me." I rubbed my sex against his cock and moved down to bite his bottom lip. "Can

I rip your panties off right now please?"

"Oh no, that would be *you* having control. I'll take my panties off when I'm ready." He groaned into my mouth as I claimed his lips with mine. I continued to tease him by rubbing against him until he could take no more. He ripped a hole in my panties, and I before I knew it, he had lifted me onto his member. We both groaned out as I impaled myself on him. My pace was quick and maddening. I hadn't realised how much I needed to fuck him until that moment. My bra was quickly removed and Alex's lips were on my nipples, teasing them with his tongue and teeth.

"That's it, Baby. Fucking ride me!" He groaned, lifting up to meet my thrusts. "Fuck, I'm so close!"

"Wait for me," I panted. "I'm almost there, too!" Alex closed his eyes, obviously trying to stop himself from cumming. Within seconds, I felt myself begin to fall and Alex let go. I dug my nails into his shoulders, trying to calm the orgasm that was surging through every inch of my body.

We collapsed in each other's arms. We were so entangled, I couldn't see where Alex ended and I started.

"That's what I needed. I'll sleep better now," Alex sighed, kissing my forehead.

"I'll do that every night if that's what you need." *I was such a whore.*

"I might have to take you up on that offer." If I could be the calm in his storm, maybe we could get through this. The next few months were going to be a struggle, but we had each other. That was all that mattered.

CHAPTER THIRTEEN

Addiction was something I knew very little about. The only thing I'd ever been addicted to was Steel Roses. Alex's addiction was something completely different.

For two months, he'd been trying to come off the drugs and alcohol. Some days had been better than others, but he hadn't been clean for a full twenty-four hours yet. Gina and I had begged him to go to rehab and pick up where the tour left off once he got out. In Alex's head, that would have meant losing me for eight weeks while he was there, so he refused.

This was a different side of Alex and a more difficult one to watch. We were on the American leg of the tour now. Every night on stage, he was under the influence and it affected the sound of his voice. The press were quick to jump on the story, slating Alex's performances, and announcing that the old *addict* Alex was back. I tried to keep him away from all the media, but he insisted on reading it. It was a vicious circle; the media would tear him down, so Alex took the drugs and alcohol to numb the pain. I couldn't make him snap out of it.

"You've got to stop beating yourself up about this." Liv looked at me, concerned. "Alex will come around."

"What if he doesn't? What if I can't help him like I

thought I could?"

"He's under a lot of pressure. It's not like he can't function. He's still managing to get on stage each night."

"That's not the point, Liv!" I didn't want to get angry with her, but she just wasn't getting it. "Addiction is a serious thing. It could fucking kill him! The whole world is laughing at the drunk rock star on stage at the moment. How is he going to get over this? Each time he tries to pick himself up, another concert review pops up and brings him down again."

"Maybe once the tour finishes he'll get better?"

"That's four months away, Liv. God knows what state he'll be in if he's still drinking and taking drugs then!" She really wasn't getting it. "Maybe rehab is the only option."

"But he won't do that until the tour is over. Alex has made that clear to everyone. Even Shane was trying to make him see sense last week. He's just not *listening*."

"Should I be tougher with him?"

"*How?*"

"Tell him I'll leave him if he doesn't go to rehab?" The words felt so alien as they fell out of my mouth, but what else could I do? I had to make Alex listen to me.

"I think that would destroy both of you, Nat." She was right, but I was clutching at straws.

"What can I do then, Liv? I'm running out of ideas."

"It's not just down to you to fix him. He's been broken almost his whole life. We're Steel Roses fans. We know the drug abuse he's been through. He has to fight this himself. You can help and support him, but don't take all of this on your shoulders. You'll buckle under the pressure."

"I have to be there for him. It's not fair for him to fight this alone."

"He's not alone. He has *all* of us. I'm worried about you, Nat. You're taking on all his pain and stress. It's not good for either of you."

"He's my whole heart, Liv. I physically hurt when he does. That's the way we work. I'm never going to stop worrying about him or feeling his pain."

"Just promise to look after yourself, too. Remember when David used to pull you down? Sometimes I can see the same look in your eyes with Alex."

"David has nothing to do with this!" Luckily, I hadn't seen that slime ball for over five months. Rock Records must have been keeping him busy at their head office. I wasn't sure if Alex had anything to do with that or not, but it was a relief not to have to deal with his antics along with everything else. David rubbing it in about Alex's addiction was the last thing we needed. "I can't believe you would even compare them!"

"I'm just telling you what I see. You're constantly on edge and snappy. Isn't that how David used to make you feel?"

"You're just saying all this because *I'm* with Alex. I'm with your childhood crush and you hate it. I really thought we'd moved past all this before I flew you out here last year!" I don't know where all these words were coming from, but this wasn't me.

"Look at yourself, Nat. Can you hear what you're saying? I don't give a fuck *who* you are dating. I love Shane! I'm worried about *you*." Liv shook her head at me. "I'm going to get some air. I don't think this conversation is going to go anywhere." I wanted to call her back to apologize, but the words just wouldn't come out. What was I turning in to?

We were in Tampa for two nights at the moment. Sitting in a hotel bar wasn't something I usually did, but for the first time in a long time, I needed a drink. The VIP lounge was quiet, so I managed to get a corner booth all to myself. After my fourth southern comfort and coke, I thought about heading back to the hotel room to find Alex. I'd try to find Liv later to apologize. Alex had been left to his own devices for about four hours now. I had no idea what state he'd be in.

"Drinking alone?" Matt smirked down at me just as I was about to leave. I'd avoided being alone with the guy these last few months. Something about him just seemed off. "You should go and join Alex. He's on his second bottle of whiskey. It should be a good show tonight." My blood was boiling. Did Matt think this was all a joke? "What are you having?" He motioned the barman over as he slid into the booth, trapping me where I sat.

"I was just leaving."

"You can have one more drink surely? All your PA duties must be done for the day if you're drinking." I wanted to find an excuse to leave, but I didn't have one. Matt was sitting too close to me, so I tried to get a little distance between us. "Do I intimidate you or something? You've been avoiding me for *months*," he mused as the barman reached us. Matt quickly ordered drinks for the two of us. "You never seem to be able to look me in the eye or be near me."

"That's because I don't like you very much!" Drinking always made me too bold. "You've caused nothing but trouble on this tour!"

"Fuck, you're feisty. I enjoy this kind of game, though. I'm all about the chase. It's making me hard just thinking about it." *I just threw up in my mouth.*

"I can assure you that I have no intention of making you hard!" What was it with egotistical rock stars?

"That's what they all say. You must know I've had my eye on you for a while. I know you're technically Alex's PA, but I could give you so much more. You really should get to know me." Matt reached out and stroked my knee. "I'd even give you overtime riding my cock if you wanted. I'd give you double pay for that." It could have been the alcohol or just the pure anger that made me slap Matt hard across the face.

"If you *ever* fucking touch me again I'll have you arrested for sexual assault and give the press my story! I don't think your already failed career would survive that," I spat. "Now get the fuck out of my way!" Matt chuckled, rubbing his face. "I'll tell Gina, too. You'll be out of the band within seconds."

"You really shouldn't threaten me, Natasha." Matt's voice was deadly. "I'm not the sort of guy you want to get on the wrong side of." He backed away from me and stood up. My heart was hammering inside my chest as I quickly moved from the booth that he'd kept me prisoner in. "Things could end badly for you if you're not careful." The fucker was threatening me?! Who the hell did he think he was? "I'll let your attitude slide this time, but if you deny me again, things will get very difficult for you."

"Do you honestly think I'm scared of you?"

"You should be. I can hurt you and the people you love. I'd watch your step, *groupie*." Matt winked sadistically before he walked off.

I froze! *Groupie?* What did he mean by that? Did he think I'd been trying to get in with the band? Was that why he made a pass at me? Liv and I had fangirled on occasion over the last few months, but most people our age loved Steel Roses. I purposely never lead any of the band on. It was better that way when it came to protecting Alex and our relationship. Fuck! What if Matt had worked out that Alex and I were dating? I don't know how he would have, though. We were always extremely careful, and we trusted the people that knew about us. Well, we trusted *most* of the people that knew. David obviously knew about us, but Alex had threatened his job if he told anyone. Rock Records also had the girlfriend bann in the contract that he'd created. David was too career driven to jeopardize his job.

Maybe I was just being paranoid. Matt's comment might not have meant anything like that, but the asshole had still threatened me. What would I do about it, though? I couldn't tell Alex. He was too fragile. Something like this would drive him to the drink and drugs even faster. Not to mention him and Matt's friendship would be over. They didn't have much to start with, but they both seemed to have healed from the past and that was important to Alex.

I was so lost in thought that I hadn't even noticed the lift was already at the hotel suite floor.

Diego was waiting to take the lift back down as it pinged open. "Where have you been, Sweet Pea?" he asked, concerned. "Alex was looking for you earlier."

"I was just having a drink in the bar. How's he doing?"

"Not great. I'm not sure how good the concert will be tonight. He could hardly stand earlier." I nodded solemnly. "Are you okay?"

"Yeah, I'm just tired." I wasn't ready to talk to anyone about Matt yet. I needed to work things out in my head first. "I'll go and check on him." I half smiled and made my way to the hotel room.

Alex was passed out on the bed when I found him. I grimaced at the three empty whiskey bottles on the floor. Had he drunk all those *today*? As I rolled him onto his side, he giggled and spoke all slurred. "Are you trying to have your way with me?"

"Not in *this* state."

"I'll be okay after a nap." He yawned and stretched, then pulled me awkwardly into an embrace. "I was waiting for you. Where have you been?"

"Did you drink all those bottles today?" I was trying to avoid his question. "You do know you're performing tonight, right?"

"Jeez! Okay, *Mom*." Alex was teasing, but after my confrontation with Matt I wasn't in a joking mood.

"This isn't fucking funny, Alex! You're slurring your words. Do you want another shitty gig review? Everyone can laugh at the washed up rock star again. Is that what you want?"

"Nat, why are you being like this?"

"Maybe I've had enough of this shit, Alex!" I motioned towards the bottles. "You said you'd try. Not once have you tried in two months!"

"Two *months*? Is that how long you thought it would take me to recover?" I could hardly understand him with the slurring. "My addiction has lasted over twenty *years*. If you can't cope for two *months*, what chance do we have?"

"Why can't you just stop?" Tears were trickling down my face. I needed *my* Alex back. I would have confided in him about Matt and then we could have faced it together. This version of Alex was in no state to help me.

"Baby, I would if I could." He ran his hands through my hair. "I'm trying. You have to believe me. I have good and bad days, but I *am* trying."

"Just hold me until we both fall asleep." I couldn't do this right now. I was at my breaking point. All I wanted was to feel his heart beating as his arms wrapped around me. Right now, that was all that made sense to me.

Alex and I both woke up groggy. Looking at the time, I panicked. We needed to be at the arena in an hour.

"Shit! Alex, we've got to get ready. The car is picking us up in ten minutes to take us to the show."

"Just a few more minutes," he sighed, pulling me towards his chest.

"We don't have any spare time," I giggled, squirming out of his hold. "Get your sexy arse up!" Throwing some clothes at him, I urged him to get changed.

I barely had time to straighten my clothes and brush my hair before Shane was knocking on the door.

"Is he ready?" Shane asked as I peered around the door.

"Almost. We'll meet you by the lift." Turning back to look at Alex, I noticed him trying to find a bottle of whiskey that wasn't empty. "Do you really need a drink right now? Maybe try some water?"

"I need it to clear my head. Water won't help!"

"We don't have time to get you a bottle right now. I'll run out and get some once we're at the arena." Was this what my life was turning into these days? Feeding Alex's addiction? He nodded and followed me down to the car.

The rest of the band was already there and had started

sound check when Alex and I arrived.

"Are you ever going to be on time?" Cody asked over the microphone. "You look like shit again, man!"

"I'll just quickly freshen up, then I'll be okay," Alex called before he turned to look at me. "Four bottles of bourbon should do it. Can you be quick please?" *Four?* Surely he didn't need them all for tonight? Like the good little PA that I was, I nodded and went to the nearest liquor store.

Watching Alex perform was becoming difficult for me. I found myself in the green room rather than at the side of the stage lately. It hurt watching him fall apart by missing his cue or forgetting the words and letting the crowd sing them instead. Part of him must not have realized he was falling from grace again. Six months ago he was the king on that stage. Now even Matt was over shadowing him with his guitar solos.

I was sitting on the couch nursing a cup of tea in the green room when Diego came rushing in.

"Jesus! Save me. Cody has gone and let Victoria backstage for the after party!" I looked at him in confusion. Who the hell was Victoria? "She's their crazy superfan! The woman is unhinged. And don't even get me started on her fashion sense!" he continued.

"Alex has never mentioned her," I chuckled. "She can't be that bad."

"You wait until you meet her. She's had this deluded idea since the eighties that her and Alex are soul mates."

"Isn't that most fans?"

"Come to the after party and see what I mean."

"I'm not really in the partying mood, Diego." I sighed,

rubbing my eyes that had suddenly gotten really tired.

"It'll be fun. You can't spend this whole tour looking after Alex. You need some fun yourself." An hour wouldn't do any harm. I had to admit, I wanted to see what this Victoria was like.

The band hadn't arrived yet. The after parties were never that busy. It was usually around fifty people that knew the band or someone connected to the band.

Scanning the crowd, I spotted who could only have been Victoria. Even I knew green and yellow should never be worn together. Yet there she was, trying to make her yellow trousers and bright, lime green top work. She might not have looked so ridiculous if she hadn't been wearing a pink bandana on her head, too. Had this girl even looked in the mirror when she left the house this morning?

"Oh dear god," I laughed, looking at Diego. "Is that her?"

"Yep, the eighties throwback! Fucking hell...are those *yellow* trousers?"

"You should go and offer her your expertise?" Diego snorted at my comment. "You could at least give her a colour chart or something so she can learn not all colours work together. Maybe she's colourblind?"

"I believe she does it to try and stand out," Diego mused. "But some people will always be plain no matter how hard they try. Not many females have natural and inner beauty like you, Baby Cakes." Diego kissed my cheek. "Now, are you going to tell me what's troubling you?" How did he know? Was I too easy to read?

"W...What do you mean?"

"You've been on edge all day. This isn't about Alex, either. Has David done something again? I've not seen you this shaken

160

up since the confrontation with him a few months back." I was about to reply, but the commotion from the band arriving took my attention. How drunk was Alex? He could hardly stand. "Nat! He can look after himself," Diego called as I made my way to Alex.

"He can hardly fucking stand!" I called back. Anger soared through me at the sight of Matt moving to hand Alex another drink while he smirked at me.

"I think he's had *e-fucking-nough*," I seethed, knocking the drink out of Matt's hand before he could give it to Alex.

"Who do you think you are? His mom?" Matt was goading me. If he wanted a fight he was going to get one.

"Why is it always you supplying him the drink and drugs? It's like you *want* him high or slurring all the time!"

"What are you trying to say?" Matt's eyes were deadly intent on me. "I'm just trying to have some fun with my *friend*."

"H...he has a point, Nat," Alex slurred, trying to hold himself upright. He was defending Matt. I couldn't stand there and witness that!

"You want to get wasted with Matt? Be my fucking guest! I'm *done*." Alex tried to call after me. I took comfort in knowing that he could barely stand so he wouldn't be able to follow me.

Diego, however, was by my side the moment I was out of the room. "Can you explain what the fuck just happened?"

"Can you please go and keep an eye on Alex? I can't do this right now!"

"Bitch! I will check on him once I know you're okay. Do *not* order me around." He was joking with me, but it still made me cry. Could I confide in Diego? I needed to talk to *someone*. "Cupcake, talk to me. What's going on?" He pulled me in for a tight hug.

"I think Matt knows about Alex and I," I whispered into his neck. Diego flinched while hugging me.

"What makes you think that?"

"He made a comment about me being a groupie and tried to hit on me. I'm pretty sure he's got Alex hooked on drugs and alcohol on purpose, too."

"Let's go and talk somewhere more private. Matt might have spies." Did Diego believe me?

We found a small bar not too far from the hotel and sat in a secluded booth while I began to pour my heart out to Diego.

"How the hell did he find out?" Diego mused.

"You think I'm right?"

"I've been having similar thoughts since the truth or dare night when Matt made you and Alex kiss. I didn't want to say anything with Alex the way he is at the moment." Diego was thoughtful before he continued. "We've all been so careful. I don't understand how he could have found out, though."

"I don't know, but I'm starting to wonder if he came back to the band because of it."

"David!" Diego gasped. "The guy is still in love with you. What if he told Matt and hoped Alex would never find out and fire his ass?" It was plausible. None of us had seen David for a while. Come to think of it, I hadn't seen him since Matt had rejoined the band.

"It makes sense, but Matt and David don't run in the same circles."

"Sweet Pea, they are both in the music industry. You'd be amazed how people can be connected."

"What do we do now? How do we find out?" Did we go

after David? Perhaps throwing Matt out of the band would be better first?

"We need to tell Alex." Diego sighed. "But we need to get the fucker clean first." That was going to be easier said than done.

Diego went back to the after party to collect Alex. Shane had been keeping an eye on him and made sure Alex didn't drink anything else.

Whatever Alex had been drinking tonight, it made him giggly. Everything was funny to him. I would have found it adorable if I wasn't so angry with him.

"Your eyelashes are curly," Alex mused, almost poking me in the eye as he tried to touch them.

"How about you try not to give me a black eye while I'm getting you ready for bed?" I teased, kissing his forehead.

"You're a funny girrrll." I didn't mind fun-loving, drunk Alex. It was the other versions that were hard to deal with. "Matt said you looked pretty today. I think he's got a crush on you."

"I wouldn't pay too much attention to Matt, Alex," Diego called from across the room. "You know he's always been full of shit."

"Are you saying Nat isn't beautiful?" Alex gasped, putting his hands on either side of his face, trying to look more shocked.

"Not at all. You know I think she's gorgeous. You need to stop trusting him so much."

"What do you mean? He's my friend!"

"You rest up. We'll talk more in the morning." Diego shook his head, rolling his eyes at me. Alex was too much for both of us at times.

"Diego is right. Get some rest. You've got a difficult few weeks ahead." Alex looked up at me, confused.

We had two weeks until we moved on to the next part of the tour. Diego, Shane, and I had all decided it was time to intervene. Alex was going to have to get himself clean in two weeks so we could finally tell him what was going on.

It was going to cut me deep watching him come down, but if he wasn't going to go to rehab we had no other choice.

CHAPTER FOURTEEN

Shane was trying to restrain Alex. It was only day one and Alex had been desperate all morning to be let out so he could get his next score. He hadn't tasted alcohol for almost twelve hours, though, and that was a start. In my mind, we just needed to get the first twenty four hours out of the way and his addiction might start to dull. I was so naive.

"Why are you doing this to me? I'm a prisoner in my own fucking hotel room!" Alex pleaded with us. "It burns! I'm itching everywhere! I can't fucking come down like this!" None of us answered him. "Let me out, motherfuckers! I hate you all!" How could he say that? We were trying to help him.

"Hey, asshole!" Diego called towards him. "You can't carry on like this! You're killing Nat and the rest of us. You need to get your head straight! You've got two weeks to wrap your head around this!"

"I was going to do all that *after* the tour, motherfucker!" I'd never seen Alex so angry.

"I've heard all that before. Every world tour you've ever done it's taken you *months* to get clean after. Fuck, most of this decade you've been high! We're trying to save you. You could lose everything. Even Nat!" Alex's eyes darted to mine as Diego yelled at him.

"You're thinking about leaving me?" The torture in Alex's voice felt like poison dripping into my veins. "Straight Lace, you promised…"

"I'm not going anywhere, but *this* has to stop. I can't watch you self-destruct for another second. I know this is painful, but please do this for me."

"I…I didn't realize I'd become so out of control." Alex reached out his arms to me. Each step I took towards him felt like coming home. Soft eyes full of love with a hint of pain behind them gazed up at me. This was *my* Alex. Was he coming back to me slowly? "I'll try, but this isn't going to be easy when I leave this room in a few weeks."

"We'll take it one day at a time. We know this isn't going to be easy for you, but we're all here to help."

"Are you going to babysit me?"

"We're just all keeping an eye on you. Not everyone around you has your best interest in mind," Diego commented. "Once you've finished this come down, you'll feel better. "

"I don't get why you guys are doing this now, though. Wouldn't it have been easier to do an intervention once we were all back in LA rather than a hotel in Tampa?"

"We'll explain all that once your head is clearer," I soothed, running my hands through his hair. I hadn't seen Alex's hair this long in a while. He'd kept it pretty short in the years I'd known him. This style was more like the old Steel Roses days.

"I'm really tired. I might try to sleep."

"Maybe when you wake up you can try some food?" Alex nodded, kissing my forehead before walking to the bedroom. "I'll even get some of your favorite chocolate."

"I might need something stronger than that." I knew he

wasn't teasing. It was going to be a difficult few weeks.

Alex didn't ask many questions during the time we were in Florida. When it was time to fly to Oakland for the next leg of the tour, he was in good spirits considering what he'd been through in such a short amount of time. The physical pain he'd endured hurt me the most. His body craved the drugs and alcohol so much that he would spasm for minutes at a time. The cries of pain were deafening and something I would never be able to get out of my mind.

I'd rung ahead and told the charter company to make sure no alcohol was served on the private jet. The rest of the band had gone a few days earlier, so we didn't have to worry about Matt supplying him with drinks this time.

I sat opposite Alex, watching his right leg shake as he looked out of the plane window.

"You're doing great," I smiled, knowing that he was panicking on the inside. "Four days clean is an amazing achievement."

"I'm still craving my next hit, though, Straight Lace. What if I can't resist? I could go straight to a dealer?"

"You're stronger than that and you know it."

"I don't know who I am in the music world without it, Nat. What if I get on that stage tonight and I can't perform because I don't have the adrenaline that it gives me?"

"You were doing it just fine before you started drinking again. The drugs don't define who you are, either. You didn't become Alex Harbour because of your addictions. You are an amazing singer and songwriter. You've given so much of yourself to your fans. That's why they love you so much."

"How do you still see so much good in me after everything you've witnessed these last few days?"

"You *are* good, Alex. I've become a better person since knowing you. Look at what you've given me...going on tour with Steel Roses, seeing the world, watching you perform every night from the side of the stage. I've dreamt of this since I was a little girl. You've given me a life I thought I could only imagine."

"Really?" Alex looked in awe at what I'd just told him. "You still feel that way even after my actions the last few months?"

"Yes, and I will feel this way every day for the rest of my life because I get to spend it with you."

"Fuck, Straight Lace. How did I ever win you?" I giggled and slid onto his lap. It was bold of me, but the cabin crew were nowhere to be seen.

"I think we both won, Alex," I whispered, pressing my lips against his. Alex deepened the kiss, holding the back of my neck. We were both breathless when we finally broke apart.

Maybe now was the time to tell him about Matt. He seemed calmer and his head was definitely in a better place.

"Diego, I think Alex is ready to be told," I sighed.

"Ready to be told what?" Alex asked, still holding onto me tightly. I slid off his lap and took the seat opposite him again. Diego moved a bit nearer, as did Shane.

"The real reason we made you go cold turkey..." Diego took a deep breath. "Matt is sabotaging you."

"What do you mean?" Alex tried to laugh it off.

"He knows about us, Alex. I'm sure of it." My voice was so quiet I hardly recognized myself.

"What? How? Why do you think that?"

"He's threatened me." Rage covered Alex's face as I continued. "He tried to make a pass at me and then said he'd hurt those I loved if I turned him down again. He's been supplying you with drinks on purpose. I'm pretty sure it was Matt who spiked your drink with drugs in the first place. He's even called me a groupie. How would he know all that if he didn't know about us? It all makes sense."

Alex was working it all out in his mind. "That motherfucker! Here I was thinking he was offering me friendship like in the old days. Buying each other drinks, taking it in turns to call our dealers and get some good shit in. Why couldn't I see what he was doing?"

"He had you under the influence just enough so you couldn't see it. He knows how your addiction works like we do." Diego smiled at him sadly. "We couldn't tell you all this while you were still high. That's why we had to do what we did."

"No, I don't blame any of you. I'm thankful. I couldn't see what was happening right in front of me. What are we going to do with the motherfucker? Right now, I want to fucking kill the fucker! Did he touch you?" Alex suddenly asked, alarmed. He was looking right at me. "I swear to god, if he touched a fucking hair on your head, he's dead!"

"No," I hushed. "I'm fine, Alex. You know I can look after myself where rockstars are concerned."

Alex smirked at me. "Yeah, that's true, but if he comes near you again, I'll fucking finish him!"

"You don't have to protect me all the time. I'm not as vulnerable as you think I am."

"I know you can hold your own, but that doesn't stop me wanting to look out for you. I haven't been doing that this month and I regret it." Alex looked tortured as he spoke.

"Stop that," I soothed, touching his chest. "You lost yourself for a bit, but that doesn't mean you have to keep blaming yourself."

"That's what I do."

"It's also how you feed your demons. We're fine, stop overthinking everything."

"You need to listen to her, Alex," Diego butted in. "She's smarter than you." Alex and I both laughed at that. It was true though.

Once we landed, we were swiftly taken through the airport away from all the fans that had gathered outside.

"How do they find out our landing times?" Shane rolled his eyes. "If it was those fucking stewardesses again I'm going to bann them on the flights."

"You know how the hysteria gets once they get back on home soil. Steel Roses was formed here. America is part of its roots." How Diego was walking and talking so quickly in those heels he was wearing still amazed me.

"Good old Oakland. It does feel like a hometown to me," Alex replied thoughtfully. I'd forgotten that's where the band got their big break. They'd been busking in Oakland when Gina noticed them. She'd been looking for something different for months—a new sound and look. Gina described seeing Alex singing on the streets like a bolt of lightning. She knew he was set for stardom by the way he held the crowd that day. Of course Alex being Alex, it took a lot to talk him around, but once he realized it wasn't some scam he and the rest of the band agreed to sign up. The moment Alex hit that first note in the recording studio everything changed. Rock Records offered them a three album deal and the rest was history.

"Did you want to go busking for a bit?" Diego teased.

"Maybe later. We've got more important things to do right now." Alex's voice was serious as we made our way out of the airport.

It didn't take long until we were on our way to the venue. Alex was sitting in the back of the car tapping his fingers on his knee.

"Are you going to be able to keep your cool with Matt when we get there?" Diego asked, concerned.

"Yeah, I've had to pretend to like the fucker for over twenty years. I'm sure a few more months won't hurt until we work out what we're doing."

He had wanted to go in guns blazing, but we'd managed to convince him that we needed proof that Matt knew about Alex and me first. That way, we knew David must have told him. It wasn't going to be easy, but using me as bait might just work.

The band was rehearsing as we entered the arena. Liv had flown in to meet them a few days ago, but knew what was going on. She had gone back to Alex's Hollywood mansion to look after Ralph with Mary over a week ago. Diego had his panties in a twist because he hadn't seen his boy for four weeks.

Liv ran straight in Shane's arms the moment she saw him. I loved how well suited she and Shane were. I really was happy she'd found a decent man.

"About time. They've been driving me crazy!" Liv motioned towards the band, then looked at Alex. "You look much better."

"It's amazing what being clean for a few days can do." He

winked at her. Liv did her fan girl giggle that she really should have grown out of by now. "How has Matt been?"

"His usual annoying self. He's been asking about you."

"I bet he has, the motherfucker." Alex turned to me. "Time to play the game," he smirked before making his way up towards the stage.

He was quite the actor. I was gobsmacked watching him with Matt while they rehearsed. He used to tell me about the part he had to play in the band, and I was beginning to see what he meant. The showman on stage wasn't the Alex I knew and loved.

"Fancy a beer now, man?" Matt asked Alex, wiping his face with a towel.

"Nah, I'm going to hit the gym. We've got to give Oakland a performance of a lifetime. We owe a lot to them." Matt looked at him, shocked. "Did you want to join me at the gym?"

"No, I'd rather get pissed in the bar with the groupies."

"To each their own, man." Alex was playing it so well. I couldn't have been prouder.

"Did you detox while we've been here?" Matt mused. "I thought rehab had you in for two months at a time?"

"I didn't go to rehab, I just decided I wanted to be clean again."

"*Why?*" Matt was trying to play it calm, but rage filled his eyes. "You love that side of this lifestyle."

"Yeah, I'm just not feeling it at the moment." I tried to hold in a giggle at Matt's stunned face. *Yes, fucker, your plan isn't working anymore.* "I want a clear head for the rest of the tour. After all, it ends in two months and then we go back to our everyday lives. I want to remember this."

"Don't you want to go out the way we started, though?"

Matt was clutching at straws.

"Yes, but it should be about the band. Our music is fucking art! We need to give these songs the justice they deserve. We owe that to our fans." *Why were my inside starting to burn? Did Alex realize how sexy he looked right now? White, he's fucking Alex Harbour, of course he knows!*

"When you put it that way, I can't argue." Matt was going down!

"Come hit the gym with me then. Cody. Masen, let's all go! We'll be pumped for later." The band couldn't argue with his plan. *He was playing this perfectly.*

Alex and I were in his dressing room. We had about an hour until show time. The support band had just gone on. The rumble of the fans was sending tremors through the building. It was going to be a loud crowd tonight.

"I don't want you leaving my side these next two months, do you hear me?" Alex murmured against my neck. "I don't want Matt alone with you."

"You know I can't do that. The only way we'll catch him is if he thinks he's got me alone."

"I can't bear the thought of him touching you."

"Two more months, then all this will be over," I soothed, wrapping my arms around his neck so I could look up at him. *Why was I getting horny now? He was due on stage soon.*

"I know that look, Straight Lace." His eyes were hungry as he gazed down at my lips. "I want to fuck you in here, but not yet. Once I finish the set tonight, I'm going to bring you back here. You're going to take a shower with me and I'm going to fuck you until you forget your own name." *Fuck, I think I just came!* "Is that okay with you?" The fucker was mocking me! I loved this playful, arrogant side of him.

"Oh, I think I'd like that a lot, but on one condition." I fluttered my eyelashes at him, trying to look as sexy as I could.

"What? You can have anything."

"I want to suck your cock here, right now." *Two can play that game, Alex!*

"Holy fucking shit...yes." His jeans were down before I even had time to blink. He must have liked the idea a lot. Alex was definitely ready for me as I gazed down.

I licked my lips in anticipation before kneeling in front of him. I was wearing a low cut top so I knew he'd have a good view of my cleavage as I knelt. I'd locked the dressing room door so we wouldn't be interrupted.

Tracing my fingertips up his calves and over his thighs, I parted his legs and moved my fingers to take his cock in my hand.

"Fuck, Baby, just start already!"

"Am I teasing you?" I knew I was, but I'd never felt so powerful.

After a few minutes of teasing, I wrapped my mouth around him and set a maddening pace, grazing my teeth gently as I sucked. The noises coming from Alex's mouth only spurred me on more, and before I knew it he had cum. I'd never been one to swallow cum, but this was *Alex Harbour*. Weirdly, I drank it like it was some fine nectar.

Alex was still trying to regain himself as I leant over and took a sip of his bottle of water.

"You are a fucking dangerous woman," he chuckled, taking me by surprise when he pulled me up onto his lap. "I better put my cock away so I can get on stage and come back for my shower."

"I can't wait."

"Make sure you're at the side of the stage tonight. I need to be able to see you." I nodded as he pecked my lips. Once he'd sorted his jeans out, he made his way to the stage.

Liv and Diego were already waiting for me when I got there. The band was due in ten minutes. The crowd was deafening, chanting out Steel Roses and Alex's name.

"I think it's going to be a crazy one tonight," Diego shouted. "I can tell by the noise."

"I hope so. Alex needs a good review. I think it will really help his progress. He seems really pumped for it, too." My eyes meet his from the other side of the stage. I'd never tire of seeing him in his legendary faded blue jeans and white vest. Cody was saying something to him, but his eyes were fixed on mine. If I had ever doubted his love for me, it would have faded with that gaze.

The arena fell silent as the band made their entrance. Alex always waited until the band had played the intro of *Free Me*—Steel Roses first ever number one—before taking his place. Everyone seemed to be screaming his name.

As Mason finished the last beat of the drum, Alex appeared on stage. One single light fell on him and the whole arena erupted. This was his night; I could feel the electricity in the air.

"Oakland! Are you ready to rock?" Alex screeched down the microphone. Even Diego and I were cheering. *I was born to rock!* "Let's fucking rock, then!" He motioned for Matt to start his guitar solo and everyone began bouncing and jumping to each beat.

On the side of the stage, I realized just how lucky I was to be a part of this...to be a part of Alex's life. I wanted this moment to last forever. I could feel everyone letting go and allowing the band to take them on the music experience of their lives. This was what Steel Roses meant to people—pure, blissful escapism.

CHAPTER FIFTEEN

I was pressed so hard against the glass that I could feel it's coldness against my cheek. The heat of the shower jets and Alex's hand greedily running over my body kept me warm, though. Of course, he'd kept to his word about fucking me in the dressing room after the show.

"Does that feel good?" he whispered into my ear, pulling my hair to make my head tilt back. His fingers were slowly rubbing my sex and it was driving me insane.

"Y...Yes." I could barely get my words out.

"I'm going to fuck you from behind like this. I wish I had a mirror out there so I could see your tits pressed against the glass." He could be such a dirty fucker. "I bet they look fucking beautiful."

"Ugh! Just fuck me, Alex!" I pleaded, forcing my butt back towards his cock.

"Oh, is someone desperate for my cock?"

"You know I am," I half laughed. "Please! Give it to me." Within seconds he was inside me, thrusting deep and fast. I tried to find something to hold on to, but the glass was too slippery. Alex's fingers dug into my hips as he pounded me as quickly as he could. I began to build within seconds. When we came, it was almost together.

"Do you remember your name?" he chuckled in my ear once we'd both come down from our climax.

"No," I snorted. "I think I'm called Doris."

"You don't look like a Doris. In Fact, I don't think I've ever fucked a Doris before," he teased as I stood up and turned around to wrap my arms around his neck.

"I should think not. Most Doris's I know are grannies."

"Grannies love me, too."

"Everyone loves you."

"I love this ass." Alex smacked my butt hard, before gripping it firmly. "We better head to the after party soon. Diego can only cover for us for so long."

"As long as you've finished groping my ass, I'm good to head off."

"Give me a minute." I slapped him playfully as he squeezed my butt a bit more. "Okay. Okay. Let's get ready." I nodded. We really both needed to get to the party.

Matt was surrounded by groupies when we arrived. The moment they spotted Alex they rushed towards us.

"I'll leave you to it," I murmured as I was pushed out of the way by three quite scary looking groupies. One, I noticed, was Victoria, the eighties throwback queen. She really got around. How did she afford to follow the band like she did?

"Don't go too far," Alex called, signing the first two posters that were thrust in his face.

"Your friend is here again," I called towards Diego, motioning at Victoria.

"I don't understand how she gets in. It's like I turn and bam…there she is in her hideous fluorescent pink outfit."

"Are the ruffles making you itch?"

"Baby Cakes, ruffles haven't been in style for twenty years, and I'm pretty sure that skirt she is wearing was made from my nan's curtains."

I was still chuckling at Diego when Matt walked over to join us. "Alex was in really good form tonight."

"That's what happens when he's not under the influence." Diego's tone was clipped. "It's funny how he only ever falls off the wagon when he's around you."

"What are you trying to say?" Matt looked offended.

"You know what I'm saying. Stop offering him drinks. If he wants one, he'll make up his own mind."

"You're quiet tonight, Nat." Matt turned his attention to me. "Is it something I said?"

"Not at all, Matt. I've been busy sorting out Alex's calendar. He's very busy once the tour finishes."

"Is that so? With what?"

"Mostly sponsors wanting him to be the face of their new brand." I was rubbing it in because I knew Matt never got offers like that. "He's going to have quite a tough decision picking which ones to go with."

"It's that pretty face of his," Diego sighed. "I'd plaster that shit everywhere because you know it's going to sell."

"Yeah, he's always been lucky with that face." Matt was trying to keep it light, but you could see the annoyance in his eyes as he downed his beer.

"How are things looking for you after the tour?" *Yes, motherfucker! White is going to put you in your place.* "Have you had many offers?"

"I don't have a PA like you that can sort all that shit for me, but I have a few deals in the works. One especially could be quite entertaining. It's with an acquaintance of mine that I've met through Rock Records." Why did I feel like he was talking about David?

"Really? It sounds very interesting."

"Oh, it will be if it goes the way I want it to," he smirked. Matt really thought he had the upper hand and I had to hide my laugh. He had no idea how strong Alex and I were. I wasn't Vanessa. I was Alex's soulmate.

"That just sounds creepy, Matt. You are a weird fucker." Diego grabbed my hand. "Baby Cakes and I need to mingle. You go and find a groupie to fuck. Victoria is over there. I'm sure she'd give you a go." Diego had dragged me away before Matt could even reply.

"Did that seem like he was talking about Alex and I?" I asked once we were far enough away.

"Yes, and I think you're right about David, too. It's time to get Gina involved. We need to cover all bases and make sure those fuckers aren't up to anything."

"Do you think they're up to something bad?"

"It depends. Matt is famous for going to the press with the smallest stories. David might be using him to spill the beans about Alex and you without getting his hands dirty. And Matt would be all in; it would give him some limelight for a few weeks." Matt was capable of that? I hadn't even thought that might have been what David was up to! "Alex is aware. We talked about it while you were asleep the other night. He's got it covered."

"How?"

"Whatever plan Matt and David have won't work because

they don't know he's going public about you in eight weeks anyway."

"Eight weeks?" I knew Alex wanted to go public after the tour, but I didn't realise it would be straight after.

"He knows you're ready." Was I? Well, I was as ready as I'd ever be.

"Why hasn't he told me?"

"He just needs some time to make sure everything is in place." I had no idea what that meant, but I trusted Alex.

After Alex's first performance in Oakland the press loved him again. It always amazed me how fickle the media could be. The write ups explained how alive he was on stage and raved that the front man was back in fine form. Diego and Liv would read the reviews out loud to the band just to spite Matt.

The tour was reaching its end, and even with all the problems, it seemed bittersweet to Liv and me. The year had passed in a whirlwind, but for fans like us it had been the experience of a lifetime.

The last show was in New York in three weeks' time. Madison Square Garden was to be Steel Roses' final send off. We were currently in Dallas, Texas. The band had one more show down here before we moved on to Washington D.C. Today was a rest day, though, and Alex had planned a fun-filled day for us.

"Horses?" I questioned, looking at the ranch. I hadn't ridden since I was ten.

"I thought it might be a nice change from riding my motorbike." Alex had a playful look in his eye.

"Do you even know how to ride?" He'd never mentioned it.

"No, but it can't be that hard." This was going to be

hilarious.

My stomach was hurting from all the laughing. It appeared that Alex wasn't quite the rider he thought he was. After three attempts, he managed to get on the horse, but the horse didn't really want to obey Alex's commands.

"You need to be more firm with the reins," I chuckled, making my horse trot over to him.

"How are you making it do that?"

"You pull the reins like this." I showed Alex. "You still have to stir them, but gently."

"I think I prefer riding my bike."

Chuckling, I carried on down the path with my horse. Alex tried to follow me as best he could. In his defense, he did seem to have quite a spirited horse, though. It didn't matter that he couldn't ride that well. I was touched that he'd even come up with the idea. I'd only mentioned my horse riding years to him once.

As we carried on along the path, I noticed what looked like a picnic blanket and hamper not too far in the distance. Had Alex arranged all this?

"Fucking finally," Alex called behind me. "I've been dying to get off this horse!"

"Did you organize all this?"

"I might have." He grinned, making his horse go faster so he could overtake me. So now he could suddenly ride? I made my horse speed up, trying to catch him.

The picnic spread was beautiful. It was full of my favorite cured meats, cheeses and crusty bread. Not to mention Cadbury's chocolate.

"I'm sorry there isn't any champagne. I can usually watch

you drink it, but didn't want to chance anything at the moment."

"No need to explain. This is perfect. You even remembered the chocolate." I beamed as he poured me some more orange juice.

"I realized we haven't had many moments like this on the tour. Being able to take a step back and enjoy ourselves is important."

"I've enjoyed every moment. We've had our alone time in the hotel suits."

"I promised to show you the world, though, Straight Lace. All I've shown you is hotel rooms and back entrances."

"You've got a lifetime to show me the world. You didn't have to do it all in one year. What I've seen so far has been incredible. Watching you on that stage each night—you don't know what that means to me. When I was a little girl I used to dream of standing on that stage with you, being part of your life. Now here I am, living my own fairy tale."

"And Matt is the wicked witch with the poison apple!" I had to chuckle at that. Alex was right. "I've set a date for us to go public about our relationship. I need to know you're ready for this."

"What's the date?"

"August the twenty second." That was the date of the last concert in New York. "Don't look so worried. Nothing will ever happen to you. I'll protect you with everything that I am."

"I'm not afraid. I'm just shocked that it's three weeks away. Every fan girl is going to hate me."

"I don't think they will." I tilted my head at him, confused. "You're one of them, Nat. You understand my fanbase because you're part of it. That's what I'm going to make them see." He looked so sure of himself. "Do you know what's stopped me from drinking and trying to score these last few weeks?"

"Diego giving you the bitch brow every time you look at a bottle or at your phone?" I teased.

"Yeah, that helps," he laughed. "I don't ever want to disappoint you again. I can't bear to see that look on your face." Was he trying to tell me that I was curing him? "I'd yo-yo between the drink and drugs with little care about ever getting clean. It was so easy and I had no consequences. Then you came along, and I slipped again, no thanks to Matt, but it was different this time."

"In what way?" I was hanging on his every word.

"I felt dirty. I couldn't stand you seeing me out of control and dependent on drugs. For the first time in my life, something mattered more to me." Alex was bearing his soul. I could hardly blink in case I missed a single second. "The need for *you* outweighs my addiction."

"What are you saying…that I'm some miracle cure?" I was almost breathless.

"You could be, Straight Lace." Alex wrapped a strand of my hair around his finger before moving in to kiss my lips tenderly. "I love you. You are *so* good for me. For years I've written songs about finding my soulmate, but I never believed those words until I met you. Maybe you are my cure. All I know is that I'm a better man since having you in my life."

"I love you, too," I gasped, needing his lips against mine again. I don't know how long we kissed and cuddled in the long grass, but once the sun began to set we knew it was getting late.

"Maybe we need to get the horses home?" I suggested, resting on his chest while tracing his *Dum spiro spero* tattoo with my fingertips. "As much as I'd love to stay here all night, I don't think the horses would like it."

"Come on then. Maybe we'll have some time for stargazing once the horses are back safe." Alex had the best ideas. Stargazing sounded perfect to me.

I was doing pretty well at teaching Alex the star systems. He enjoyed stargazing as much as me. We must have sat outside the ranch for hours, trying to name as many star constellations as we could.

"We should have brought your telescope," Alex mused, watching me. I was still gazing up at the night sky. "I love how mesmerized you get by the stars."

"It's my dad's fault. I've been doing this since I was little."

"Come on. We better head back. It's getting late."

"I've had an amazing day," I grinned. It truly had been a day to remember. Just having some alone time with Alex meant so much to me.

"Me too, Baby. Once the tour is over we'll have more days like this." That sounded wonderful to me.

The hysteria was at an all-time high as the tour was coming to an end. Shane had doubled the security on the last few hotels we were staying at. We were making our way through the last of the dates now and were currently back in Florida.

"Do you think we'll have time to go to Disney World this time?" Liv asked as we relaxed by the pool.

"I don't think so. There aren't very many rest days on the last leg of the tour."

"*We* could just go. Maybe take Diego?"

"He flew back home to spend time with Ralph. I don't think he'll be back until we reach New York." Ralph had taken such a part of Diego's heart. He was the best gift Alex and I could have given him.

"I swear he'd marry that dog if he could."

"They are pretty sweet. Ralph does this cute bouncy jump at the door when Diego gets home. Diego always films it and sends it to me."

"Diego needs to find a man as crazy about dalmatians as he is." I chuckled, but Liv was right.

"Hi, ladies!" I froze at the voice behind us. What the fuck was David doing here? "I see you're enjoying the Florida sun."

"What the fuck are you doing here?" Liv seethed. "Didn't Alex make it clear enough?"

"I work for Rock Records. I'm here to check on *their* investment." I didn't believe that for a single second.

"Why don't you go and find the band instead of hassling us then?" I adored protective Liv. "You're blocking our sun!"

"My apologies." I didn't trust the smile on David's as he walked off. Liv was up on her feet the moment he left.

"Do you think he's trying to find Matt?"

"I have no idea what he's doing here. Why would Rock Records need to check on their investment when the tour is nearly over?"

"I think it's all bullshit. Let's go and find Shane. I'll get him to throw David out." I was pretty sure Shane couldn't do that, but the image in my head was great.

Alex was busy being interviewed by numerous press so I didn't have to worry about him seeing David straight away.

We split up to search for Shane. David had caught up with

the rest of the band and was having a drink with them in the bar as I wandered past.

"Nat, did you hear the good news?" Cody yelled as he noticed me walking by. "Rock Records want us to sign up for another world tour next year! Maybe the band will stay together." That was the first I'd heard of this. Had they even spoken to Alex about it?

"Really?" I gasped. "Does Alex know?"

"Not yet. I'll be chatting with him once he's done with the interviews." David looked smugly at me. "The fans clearly want more of Steel Roses and frontman Alex. Who are we to deny them?" This was his plan? To try and split Alex and I up with another world tour?

"I can't speak for Alex, but I always got the impression that he wanted to concentrate on his solo career after this tour."

"Really? You don't speak for him?" Matt questioned. "Sometimes I wonder if there is more to your relationship than just being his PA. You two are *always* together."

"I wouldn't be much of a PA if I wasn't always with him, Matt!" I snapped, crossing my arms. Luckily, the rest of the band didn't make any further comment on his remark. "I just think you need to speak to him before you start celebrating. This is all new information, after all. No contract has been signed."

"It was in the small print of the first contract," David piped up. "If the band secured enough profit, another tour might take place." That was definitely not in the contract Alex and I had seen. "Alex wouldn't go against the wishes of Rock Records, the company who *made* him, would he?"

"That would really destroy his career," Matt sighed, looking over at David. "I would hate to see Alex fall from grace like that. The guy has only just got clean again."

"That would be awful. We both think so highly of him," David sneered, smirking at Matt. We were right. David and Matt were working together, but it wasn't just about splitting us up. They wanted to destroy Alex's whole career. *Fuck! White, you need to find your rockstar...now!*

CHAPTER SIXTEEN

I sat impatiently, waiting for Alex to finish his last interview. I needed to get to him before David and Matt did. They were waiting outside the interview room with the rest of the band.

"What are your plans after the tour ends, Alex?" A young blonde reporter asked.

"Well, I'm going to find happiness. I've spent a lot of my life in the dark. I'm going to take a break from writing music for a few years and live my life."

"A few years? So, the fans can't expect any new material from you until then?"

"No. Steel Roses won't be producing any new songs, either. This wasn't a comeback tour—this was a farewell tour for the fans. A final salute, so to speak."

"That's not what Rock Records have been implying on social media today." Oh shit! Was I already too late?

"What do you mean?" Alex's eyes flashed towards mine.

"They are teasing at a possible second world tour."

Alex laughed loudly. "There might be, but I won't be front lining it. Matt has wanted the spotlight for twenty years, maybe he'll finally get his chance."

"So you're saying you won't be taking part in the second

tour?"

"I most definitely won't be." Alex looked at his watch. "We need to wrap this up. Do you have a final question?"

"Oh, yes, sorry." The reporter got a little flustered looking over her notes, trying to find a good last question. "Do you think you're over the hill yet, or is the best yet to come?" *Well, that was fucking rude!*

"In my career maybe I've reached my peak, but I'm a different man these days. Personally, I think the best is yet to come." The reporter nodded and smiled.

"Thank you for your time today, Alex. This interview will go great with tonight's gig write up. I'm excited for the show."

"No problem. I hope you enjoy yourself this evening." He shook her hand and then made his way straight over to me.

"Nat, what's wrong?" He could read my face so well. I led him out onto the balcony in the interview room so we wouldn't be disturbed.

"David is here." Alex flinched with anger. "Wait, there's more. Rock Records has sent him. Supposedly, there is some fine print in the contract that says if Steel Roses surpassed a certain amount in profits they would go on a second world tour. The tour is *next year!*"

"Fucking bullshit! That was *not* in the fucking contract! This was a one time deal!"

"David was renowned for fudging contracts at Flavour Records. I think he's done the same for Rock Records. You're probably tied to this. He knows what he's doing. I think Matt is hoping you'll drop Rock Records and destroy your career."

"Motherfuckers! Where are they now?"

"They're outside waiting for you to finish your interviews

so they can tell you the good news."

"Right, let's get this fucking sorted!"

"Please be careful," I pleaded. "Don't do anything rash!"

"Straight Lace, I'm done playing nice. These fuckers are going down!" His eyes were deadly as he looked away from me. "They think they have all the cards, but they don't."

"You can handle this then? We won't be going on tour again?" I couldn't cope with another tour, not so soon after this one. Not with Matt and David trying everything in their power to break Alex and me.

"Baby, hush." Alex stroked my face, running his fingertips across my lips. "I've got this. We won't be going on tour with Steel Roses again, I promise." I trusted him, but feared for him at the same time. I'd seen firsthand the damage David had done with artists at Flavour Records.

The band and David were all outside the room to greet him as we walked through.

"Did Natasha tell you the good news?" Matt asked with a smug grin.

"Yes. David, can I have a private word?"

"Don't you want to celebrate with your band mates first? You've made rock history. This is the biggest comeback of the decade!" The rest of the band cheered at David's comment. "Let's have a drink first!"

Cody and Masen were so excited. Alex knew he'd have to let them down gently. They still had six more shows to do and he didn't want to disappoint them until he could fully explain.

"One drink. Then we talk."

"Of course." David patted him on the back before following the rest of the band to the bar. If anything was going to test Alex and his demons, it was going to be entering that bar and just ordering an orange juice. He had been avoiding the bars for the last few months for that very reason.

I kept my distance in the bar and sat with Liv and Shane, who had already found a seat.

"What is Alex going to do?" Shane asked once I'd told them what they had missed. "Is he going to leave Rock Records?"

"I don't know. He told me it's all in hand, and that he won't be going on tour with Steel Roses again." I gazed over my shoulder. Alex was sipping an orange juice while listening to Cody and Masen chat. "I know how dirty David can play with contracts, though. I'm really worried for him. He's fragile right now with his addiction. What if this makes him slip again?"

"Then we make him go to rehab right after the tour," Liv replied. "It's only a week until the tour ends." I wasn't sure Alex even wanted to go into rehab now.

I felt like all of this was my fault. "I hate this! Why did David have to take a job at Rock Records?! Matt wouldn't have anything on Alex if it wasn't for me."

"Natty, stop," Liv cautioned me. "This is *not* your fault. You have a psycho ex that won't let you go. This is *all* on David!"

"I feel so helpless, though! I want to be stronger for Alex. He deserves that!"

"You're the strongest woman he's ever known!" Shane interjected. "And trust me, before you, he knew *a lot* of women!" Strangely that gave me a lot of comfort.

An hour later, I saw Alex pull David away for the chat. I desperately wanted to go with him, but Alex didn't even meet my gaze as they walked passed. That told me he wanted to talk to David alone. I really hoped he knew what he was doing.

The mood of the show tonight was more solemn than other nights. Alex had practically gone on stage after talking to David. I was distraught at not knowing what had transpired. Whatever Alex had said, David left straight after.

"Does he seem okay to you?" I asked Liv as we stood watching the show at the side of the stage.

"I'm not sure. His energy is weird tonight." Liv had a point. Alex seemed almost over excited on stage. He couldn't stand still. I prayed he hadn't taken anything and it was just adrenaline.

Gasping in relief as the show finished, Alex made his way straight towards me. "Let's get back to the hotel." What, no after party this time? I wasn't going to argue; I needed to know what had happened with David.

Alex had been pacing the room for ten minutes since we got back. He was trying to decide where to start.

"I can't tell you everything that was said in that room with David...not yet."

What?! "Why? What has he got on you?"

"Nothing! I promise by the end of this tour you will know everything. I want to do this all my way, otherwise it won't work. Can you trust me?"

"It looks like I don't have a choice." I pouted and Alex tilted his head, smirking. "Don't look at me like that!" I snapped.

"But you look adorable when you pout."

"I'm pissed with you! Why can't you just tell me? I won't say anything!"

"It's not about trusting you. I have things in place. I need to do this my way. Please, Straight Lace, just trust me. Trust that I have all this in hand." His face was full of love and so sincere. How could I *not* trust him?

"Okay, but please be careful." Alex pressed his lips softly against mine and inhaled. It felt as if all the tension from his body lifted the moment he kissed me.

"You know I would never do anything to jeopardize *this*. You are *everything* to me." His words had never been more true; I felt the same way. I fell into his embrace, basking in the amount of love we had for each other. Whatever came our way, we could face it together. Our love was that strong.

"Disney World?" Liv and I stood motionless, looking out towards Cinderella's castle. Shane and Alex had blindfolded us for the better part of two hours, but never in our wildest dreams did we think they'd take us here. "Are you guys for real? I thought it didn't open for another two hours!"

"Alex got us VIP status. We basically have this place to ourselves until it opens, then VIP access and an overnight stop." Liv did a high pitched scream and jumped on Shane in excitement. This was how they'd chosen to spend their days off. These guys were amazing!

"You brought us to freaking *Disney World*! You two are the best boyfriends ever!" Liv was so over excited, she was skipping around like a schoolgirl.

"Told you it was a good idea," Shane commented to Alex. This had been Shane's idea, probably because Liv hadn't stopped banging on about it.

"Come on, let's get on these rides while it's quiet." Alex

put his arm around me and I looked at him, alarmed. "It's okay, everyone here has signed a nondisclosure agreement. We can be ourselves." When did he organise all this? He'd been flat out with the tour, and I'd hardly left his side.

"How did you arrange all this?"

"I have a few contacts here. It was pretty easy to sort out." Alex smirked, kissing my forehead. "I thought a bit of *us* time would be nice for our last two days off before the end of the tour." It was scary to think Steel Roses only had two nights left, both in New York. The band seemed to think that a second tour was still in the cards. Alex had told me to keep quiet until he sorted it out. Honestly, I had no idea how he was going to sort everything in less than a week, but he'd told me to trust him, so that's exactly what I was doing.

"You already treated me when we went to the ranch," I pointed out.

"This is more Liv's treat," Alex winked, letting me get onto the ride first. "You're not afraid of heights, are you?" I really hoped I still liked roller coasters. It had been a while since I'd been on one.

Well, I definitely wasn't fifteen anymore. I spent more time holding onto Alex's arm and screaming with my eyes closed than actually enjoying the rides. I was okay if it didn't go upside down, but the ones that did scared the shit out of me. The other problem was with being the only people in the park. We got to sit in the front seats every time, which was pretty scary. I'd lost track of how many rides we'd been on, but I knew I needed a rest once I started to feel sick.

"Do you need a break from the rides?" Alex snorted. "You look a little pale."

"Yes, please. Let those crazy two carry on without us." Shane and Liv couldn't get enough of the rides and quickly disappeared.

"Do you want to go and explore the castle instead?" My eyes lit up. "I'll take that as a yes." *Keep calm, White. It's just the Disney castle!*

Every little girl dreams of seeing the Disney castle one day, but sharing my experience with my school girl Rock Star crush seemed insane. I had to pinch myself to make sure all of this was happening.

"Did you just pinch yourself?" *Fuck, did I do that for real?*

"Ummmm...I had an itch?"

"Why didn't you scratch it then?" Alex snorted. "This is all real. You don't need to keep checking."

"Today is a bit more surreal. The Rockstar and the Castle."

"Sounds like a good book." I loved funny, carefree Alex. He seemed calm, like he had everything under control.

"Maybe I'll write it one day," I giggled. It actually sounded like a great kids book!

"Come on then. Let's go and have a look around my castle." Alex entwined his fingers with mine. This was the first time we'd held hands in public, and I had to admit I liked it. It felt natural. It wouldn't be too long until we'd be doing this all the time. The countdown clock was almost done and I couldn't wait, but for now, I was going to enjoy exploring Disney World. After all, this was the place dreams could come true.

CHAPTER SEVENTEEN

In the blink of an eye the tour was almost over. After getting back from Disney World, it had all been a blur. It didn't feel like a year had gone by, but a lot of the days had merged into one. The tour had mostly involved getting on the tour bus, doing soundchecks at the venues and sleeping at hotels. Watching all the concerts from the side of the stage would always hold the most precious memories for me, though. Going on tour with a rock band hadn't been quite as glamorous as I had imagined at times, but being able to share it with Alex made it all worth it.

"Why does all the exciting stuff happen when I'm not here?" Diego had come back for the last few days. "Ralph loves a bit of gossip, too! I should've brought him along to the last leg of the tour."

"You love that dog too much to put him through that." I chuckled. "How's he doing, anyway?"

"He's great. Mary is taking good care of him at the house." I missed Mary and her cooking. It seemed like a lifetime since we'd been at the Hollywood Hills mansion.

"I can't wait to go home. This tour has really taken it out of me."

"You've been amazing, Baby Cakes! What you and Alex have faced this last year, what you've helped him fight—I'll be forever indebted to you for saving my best friend."

"He's still struggling, though. I saw him looking at the whiskey bottles last night."

"It has always been an uphill battle for him. Every day he has to fight his addiction. Just remember...you are the reason he resists. Honestly, I've never seen him this strong so quickly after a relapse."

"Do you know what his plan is tomorrow night?" Diego was Alex's closet friend. He had to know *something*.

"Are you still digging for information?" Diego tutted at me, tossing his long blonde hair behind his shoulders. "Even if I did know anything I wouldn't tell you. It's a surprise."

"I *hate* surprises." Crossing my arms, I scowled at him. "Does he realize how dangerous David can be?"

"Alex has been in this business much longer. Trust me, I think he's more dangerous."

"Do you know where he is right now?" Alex had left early this morning with Shane, but told me it was all part of the surprise.

"Maybe," he grinned. *Ugh, this was infuriating!* "I have my orders for today, though."

"Which are?"

"I'm taking you shopping for an outfit." More shopping? What was going on?

"I have enough clothes."

"No, this is an outfit for after the show tomorrow." Diego reached out to touch my hair. "We need to sort these dry ends, too. Have you been using the conditioner I gave you?"

"Yes!" I snapped, pulling the strand of hair away from his fingertips. "Anything else you want to insult? How's my skin?"

"It's a bit dry. I might call in a few favors and get some treatments booked." He was on his phone before I had time to refuse. He was impossible when he was in this kind of mood.

We went shopping first. Diego had booked us for three treatments after lunch. I didn't want to admit it, but after the week I'd had, I was looking forward to having a bit of a pamper.

"What about this?" I'd lost count of the number of designer shops we'd been in. Diego was holding up a red dress that looked quite floaty. It reminded me of Marilyn's infamous white dress that she was so often pictured in. "You look great in red."

"Why do I need a new outfit, anyway?"

"Will you stop being a brat and just cooperate?" Diego stomped. "How Alex finds that pout cute, I'll never know. It makes you look twelve." *He was such a bitch!* "No, actually it makes you look like a hooker. Maybe that's *why* he likes it." Diego was chuckling at his own comment but I didn't find him funny. "Oh, lighten up! I'm teasing."

"Okay, fine! I'll try that one on." After taking the dress from him, I made my way to the changing rooms. I know he was trying to cheer me up, but I seemed to be the only person worried about David and Matt. Whatever they were planning, it was going to play out in the next few days. There were only two more Steel Roses concerts left!

Looking at myself in the mirror, I had to admit that Diego had done it again. The dress was perfect. The top clung in all the right places and showed my cleavage off magnificently, while the skirt showcased my waist in a very flattering way.

"Stunning!" Diego gasped as I walked out to show him. "And you're smiling! That's a start."

"I like the dress."

"What about shoes? Maybe a clutch, too? I saw a nice silver on over there. You change and I'll go and have a look." *Diego and his accessories.*

Once we had the complete outfit, we went for a coffee break in Bryant Park. It was nice to get away from all the buildings and busy streets for a little while. We chose a round metal table near the coffee shack and sat for a little while, just watching the world go by.

"Why are you so worried about David and Matt?" Diego finally asked.

"I worked with David back in London. I've watched him destroy more than one Flavour Record artist. He's a very powerful man."

"And you don't think Alex is powerful?"

"If Rock Records drop him because he won't go on a second tour, what will he do? What if his career is destroyed?"

"If Alex was going to destroy his career, he would have done that in the last ten years. You know the shit he released while he was constantly high still sold. His fans will never abandon him. Rock Records *is* Alex. They may have given him his big break, but he *made* them what they are today. They've got *nothing* if they lose him. If they're stupid enough to give him a mandate, then they are signing their own death warrant." Was that really how it worked? At Flavour Records there always seemed to be another rock star ready to replace the falling one. That was the cut throat way of the industry. Nobody stayed number one forever. I didn't want to be the reason Alex slipped from the top.

"This industry can be ruthless, though. What if Rock

Records replaces him?"

"How could they replace him? He's an iconic legend!" Diego shook his head at me. "I get that you're worried—you love him. You want to protect him, but *trust* him. There is a reason he's keeping you in the dark."

Admitting defeat, I sighed deeply. "Okay, I'll drop it. I only have until tomorrow to find out anyway, I guess."

"That's my girl!" Diego praised. "Now, let's go and sort out those dry ends."

"You are such a bitch," I giggled, following him to hail a cab.

Diego must have called Liv because she was already waiting for us as we reached the beauty salon. "I love a surprise girly pamper!" she beamed, hugging me.

"Well, it's the final countdown. I think we all need a treat!" Diego ushered us into the salon.

No expense was spared. My skin was exfoliated from head to toe. Any stress or tension I had was massaged away. After a facial, my hair was treated and cut. Gazing at the face in the mirror, I hardly recognized myself. I looked so refreshed.

"Now that is much better." Diego was pleased with himself. "How about we hit the spa for an hour? We still have a little time. Maybe we can order some bubbly?" A glass of champagne did seem like a great idea.

By the time we got back to the hotel, I was a changed woman. Worrying for Aex wasn't doing me any good. Diego was right; I needed to trust that Alex knew what he was doing.

I headed up to the hotel suite first, hoping Alex would be back from wherever he had gone this morning. Walking through the door, I froze at the sight in front of me.

"La mia dolce piccolina!" My mother cried, rushing over to me. My dad was standing behind her. What the fuck were my parents doing here?

"Mum? Dad?" I questioned, confused. "What are you doing here?"

"Alex flew us over. He's such a lovely boy!" My mother was already his number one fan. I could tell.

"Hello, Natty." My dad hugged me tightly. "We've missed you."

"I've missed you guys, too." I was still totally baffled as to why they were here. They didn't even *like* rock music. "Where is Alex?"

"He's just finishing up a meeting. He should be back soon." My mother pulled me over to the sofa. "Anyway, we want to hear *everything*. How has the tour been? You look beautiful. Have you coloured your hair?"

"No, I've just had a treatment." Looking over at my dad, I tried to gage his face for any answers, but all I saw was pure joy. *What the hell are you up to Alex Harbour?!*

Alex finally got back an hour later. He was cutting it pretty close for the show tonight. He only had a few hours until we needed to head to the venue.

"What do you think of your surprise?" He smirked, motioning towards my parents. *This was the surprise?* I had to admit it had been great catching up with them. "I amaze myself sometimes."

"I...it's wonderful, but why...?"

"I know you miss them, and I wanted them to have a

glimpse into our world." Alex interrupted me. "Mr. and Mrs. White, do you mind if I have a quiet word with Nat? We have a few things to discuss."

"Oh, of course, Alex. We'll head back to our room." My mother was overly excited as she hugged Alex. My dad shook his head and gave him a weird nod. *What the hell was that about?*

"I'll have Shane come and get you once we're ready to leave for the venue," Alex called out to my parents just before they left. Turning towards me, he gave me a heart-stopping smile. "You had no clue, did you?"

"I'm a little confused. What the fuck are my parents doing here?" Alex took my hand in his and led me to the couch, where he took a seat before pulling me down beside him.

"I need you to stay calm, okay? " Oh fuck! What has happened? "Our relationship is going public in an hour." *Holy fucking shit!* Despite his request, I began to hyperventilate; I thought I still had a few days to get my head around Alex's fanbase hating me for eternity. "Straight Lace, breathe. It's okay."

"W...why today? The tour isn't over yet! Shouldn't you have asked me first?"

"We've talked about this. You knew it was going to happen. Matt has gone to the press about our relationship. The story will break tomorrow. It was always his and David's plan to leak the information on the last day of the tour. David somehow has pictures of us kissing." Oh! Now everything was starting to make sense. "I wanted to tell you, but I didn't want you to stress any more than you already are."

"How does he have pictures?" We'd been so careful.

"They could be photoshopped for all I know—I wouldn't put it past either of them—but none of that matters. We've taken the control from them by announcing it ourselves." Looking down at our entwined fingers, I smiled shyly. "You're not angry that I made the decision for us, are you? We'd already talked about going public, and truthfully, Straight Lace, I want to sing from the rooftops about you. I don't want to hide you away anymore. I want to be able to hold your hand in public, and have you by my side at every event I go to."

"I'm not angry." I didn't realize I was crying happy tears until Alex wiped a single drop trickling down my face away with his thumb. "I want all that, too. I'm not afraid anymore. All I want is you." Alex's lips crashed fiercely against mine. It felt as if we couldn't get close enough to each other. He pulled me up onto his lap and his hands tangled in my hair as we kissed, barely coming up for air.

Subconsciously, I began to grind against him. My body was calling out for him and his touch.

"We don't have long, Baby," Alex whispered against my mouth, pulling on my bottom lip with his teeth.

"We don't need long," I replied breathlessly, moving to undo his trousers. I needed him right now!

Luckily I was in a skirt; it was easy for Alex to slide my panties to the side as he entered me. We both let out a groan of pleasure at being connected this way. Nothing was more satisfying than him being inside me.

The pace was maddening. Alex had a hold of my waist and was slamming me up and down on his member.

Somehow, my breasts had escaped my top. I'd been too lost in the pleasure to remember Alex doing that. As his mouth descended on my nipples, I let out a loud groan. My orgasm was building. Every nerve ending in my body had been ignited, and I was close to losing my mind with pleasure.

"Baby, I'm close. Fucking let go. I want it all." At Alex's words, we both climaxed and fell into the abyss together.

"I love you," Alex muttered against my lips as we came down from our orgasm a while later. "It's never felt like this before."

"I love you, too," I whispered, running my hands through his hair. "Now, Mr. Rockstar, you've got a show to do." Alex's phone suddenly started pinging. We looked at the time. An hour had gone by. *Fuck! Our relationship was official!*

"Time to face the world *official girlfriend!*" He grinned, kissing my forehead. It was show time!

It took me longer to get ready to head downstairs. I knew the press would be waiting for me. Not to mention the groupies, who were probably ready to throw rotten tomatoes at me. I had to make sure I looked worthy to be on Alex's arm.

"You look beautiful. Stop worrying!" Alex called, watching me study myself in the mirror.

"I'm in jeans though! Maybe I need to put a dress on?"

"You don't need to prove anything, Straight Lace. I fell in love with the girl that constantly had her hair up in a messy bun, that usually had a stain on her top, and hated walking in heels." I hardly recalled that girl anymore. Alex had given me so much confidence these days. "Let's go." With a deep breath, I nodded and took his hand to leave.

Shane was already downstairs in the lobby with my parents and Diego. Now I understood why Alex had flown them over. It was all extra support for me.

"There are the lovebirds!" Diego called, opening his arms out to me. "I told you not to worry," he whispered in my ear and he hugged me.

"It's pretty hectic outside. I think we'll need to head out the back way," Shane suggested, signaling for a few of his men to follow us. "The cars will meet us there."

The press was at the back entrance too, trying to take mine and Alex's picture, but not as many as were probably in front of the hotel. Fangirls were crying, screaming Alex's name. I heard a few insults being yelled about me, but I'd been gearing myself for the wrath of the fans for months now.

"See, that wasn't so bad." Alex chuckled as we began to drive off. "Now we can go and see Matt's stunned face." *That* I couldn't wait for!

There were a lot of familiar faces at the venue. Milly was waiting with Naomi to congratulate us on becoming official as we arrived. I knew Alex had invited all our friends for extra support.

"How does it feel now that your dirty secret is out?" Milly teased, nudging me. "Diego filled me in on Alex's relapse. You did good. He looks amazing."

"It's been a testing time," I winced. "It feels great having everything out in the open."

"I'm happy for both of you," she winked as the rest of the band came into view. Matt couldn't even meet Alex's or my gaze.

"You two kept one hell of a secret," Cody snorted, patting Alex on the back. "You sly dog, hitting on your PA."

"We didn't want to go official until we knew it was serious. Now just seemed like the right time with the tour coming to an end." Alex put his arm around my waist, pulling me closer.

"We're made up for you guys!" Masen yelled. "Aren't we, Matt?" he asked, noticing Matt seemed a little detached.

"Oh, yeah... It's great news." *Yes fucker! You lost!* "Let's hope nothing happens to this one, hey?"

"What the fuck do you mean by that?" Alex roared, pushing at Matt's chest. "I swear to god...if you so much as look at Nat in the wrong way, I will fucking finish you!" Everyone around us looked shocked and confused at the sudden outburst.

"Come on, big man. You want to finish this right now?" Well, that escalated quickly. Matt looked like he was raging for a fight.

"Matt, calm the fuck down," Naomi cautioned. "You have to be on stage in forty minutes. Now isn't the time for this!" Cody and Masen looked at each other bewildered, watching Alex and Matt's deadly stares at each other.

"We'll finish this later, motherfucker," Alex spat, pushing him. Matt went to take a swing at him but Shane stopped him, pushing him hard so he fell on the floor.

"Didn't you listen to Alex, Asshole? You can sort your shit out *after* the show!" I'd never seen Shane get handsy with one of the band before, but Matt deserved it. He really had overstepped the mark. Everyone walked past him on the floor, not even giving him a single glance. Matt was where he belonged after that reaction.

CHAPTER EIGHTEEN

The crowd was electric tonight. It could have been the new found freedom I was experiencing that was making the night seem more magical. Alex was owning the stage, and I'd never seen him look so alive.

The guys were only a few songs into their set. My parents were at the side of the stage with me, along with Liv, Diego, Naomi and Milly. We were all dancing, singing, and jumping around, basically just rocking out to the pure talent that was Steel Roses. It made a change for Naomi to be at the side of the stage when she was usually running things below. The crew was like a well-oiled machine these days. She was an amazing tour manager.

"I can see why you liked this music now," my mother shouted in my ear. "He's very sexual on stage, isn't he?"

"Mother!" I snorted as she watched Alex gyrating his pelvis. "But yes, he's quite the showman." I could hardly believe that sexy rock star on stage was all mine.

On the guitar change, Alex came rushing over to me. My heart almost stopped in my chest watching the sweat trickle down his face as he approached. "I've been waiting fucking months to be able to do this!" I frowned and was about to reply when his lips crashed hard against mine. A roar of cheering and clapping seemed to echo around us, but I was too lost in the kiss to notice where it was coming from. *Alex was kissing me on the side of the stage!* "This next song is for you." I was in a daze as I watched Alex run back onto the stage.

"Are you rocking yet, New York?" Alex asked the crowd. A loud cheer erupted in Madison Square Gardens. "This next song you all know pretty well, but what you don't know is that I wrote it for my girlfriend, Natasha. Baby, this one's for you." As the strings began to play the first few chords to Wonderlust I felt like I was flying. Alex had dedicated a song to me! My heart burst with love at that moment. I couldn't keep my eyes off him for the rest of the show.

"That was fucking amazing, man!" Cody was bouncing around. "Did you hear that crowd tonight?"

"I'm going to miss this." Masen sighed. "One more show to go! Band hug!" Matt wasn't even paying attention to the band. He was pretending to check his guitars. "Matt?" He still didn't respond. "What the fuck happened with you two?" he asked Alex.

"I'll explain it another time." Alex addressed everyone else. "Nat and I need to sort this out with him. We'll meet you all at the party in a bit." I was getting to stay for the showdown with Matt. *Whoop! Time for some ass kicking, White!*

Matt still had his back to us after everyone had gone. "We're alone now, motherfucker. You can stop pretending you're checking those guitars!" Alex's voice was deadly. I moved to stand next to him so we presented a united front.

"I was right then," Matt seethed. "You've been fucking the

PA this whole time."

"Don't try and be clever. I know everything. David Barcley told you about us because he's as bitter and twisted as you are." Matt looked at him, alarmed. "Yes, motherfucker, I know *everything.*"

"I don't know what you are talking about!" Matt was stressing, I could tell.

"How much did you sell our story for? Fifty grand or more?"

"I'd never sell a story on you, man. Come on! I've known you twenty years."

"And hated me for all of them. This is done, Matt. You can't break Nat and me up, we're stronger than that. We have something you'd never understand."

"YES I WOULD!" Matt yelled at the top of his lungs, taking us both by surprise. "I had that with Ness! You fucking took her from me! I won't rest until I've taken Nat from you! Next tour, I'll fucking break you two piece by fucking piece. Every chance I've got, I'll ruin the pair of you."

"Can you hear yourself?" I seethed. With Alex by my side I felt strong. I could take this fucker down! "No one likes you in the band, Matt. It was nice when you left. Max did a much better job than you. It took him an afternoon to learn all your solos! You think you're this important member of the band, but you're not. The groupies only fuck you beacaue you know *Alex.* They scream because you're in *Steel Roses.* Alone...you are fucking *nothing!*"

"What the fuck do you know?"

"I used to *be* a fucking groupie, asshole! If you think Alex and I are intimidated by a pathetic little weasel like you, you're delusional!" Matt lunged at me but Alex was in his face in an instant.

"Fucking try it, I dare you!" Alex goaded him. "Give me a reason to smash that fucking face of yours! A black eye will look good for the last show, don't you think?"

"How do you always come out on top?" Matt pushed back, stepping away from us. "Every fucking time! You never lose anything! It eats me up inside that you have never paid for the damage you've done."

"I've done my time, Matt. I spent ten years slowly killing myself until I met Nat. This feud ends here. Do you understand?"

"And what if I can't let go?"

"Then there will be consequences. I'm giving you a choice, so don't fuck this up." Matt looked down at the floor but moved closer to Alex and offered his hand to shake. Surely it couldn't be that easy?

Alex reached out, but just before their hands touched, Matt pulled back and spat in Alex's face. "FUCK YOU AND YOUR WHORE! I'LL DESTROY YOU BOTH ON THE SECOND TOUR!" Everything happened in a blur. Matt lunged out to hit me, but Alex swung a punch first, hitting him square in the face. Matt fell to the floor. It looked like Alex had broken his nose. There was blood everywhere.

"We're fucking done here. Come on, Straight Lace." Alex sighed sadly. "You can't save everyone." Those couldn't be truer words. Now the only thing I was worried about was how Alex was going to get out of the second world tour. He hadn't explained that to me yet. We walked away, leaving Matt bleeding on the floor.

"How did it go?" Liv asked as we arrived at the party. It was pretty busy and I could see a few press already looking our way.

"I think Alex broke Matt's nose," I snorted.

"No fucking way!" Liv's eyes widened in shock. "Alex *actually* hit him?"

"He probably deserved it," Diego muttered. "That fucker needed taking down. I wish I'd been there to see it, though! I haven't seen Alex punch Matt since two thousand and one."

"It's over now. After tomorrow, we'll have nothing more to do with him." Alex draped his arm over my shoulders. Taking a deep breath, I relaxed into him. The worst was over. We had one night of the tour to go and Alex had everything in hand. Tomorrow night wouldn't be as eventful as tonight; I'd rest easy knowing that fact.

Matt had quite the black eye when he surfaced for breakfast the next morning. He didn't even speak to Alex or me.

As I had thought, I'd slept like a log and felt really refreshed. Last night hadn't been too bad. The press had questioned us a little, but it was nothing too invasive. It was mostly how we'd gotten together and how long we had been dating. Alex had been his usual calm self, taking it all in his stride.

"Did you want any more juice?" He smiled sweetly at me.

"No, I'm good, thanks."

"Have you noticed his shiner?" He motioned towards Matt sitting on the table at the far end of the room. "I think he'll need a fair bit of makeup to hide that."

"I'm surprised he even came down to have breakfast."

"He's probably hoping to get some sympathy from the other members. I've told them the truth so he won't get any."

"Did you speak to them about the second tour?" David

destroying his career was still playing on my mind.

"Yeah, they know my plans. They're good with it. I haven't said *never*, but if it does happen, it will be without Matt and on *my* terms."

"How did they take it?"

"Fine. They've never been attention whores like Matt. For them, it's about the music. They are the true musicians. Besides, we've all made enough money on this tour to last a long time." That went easier than I thought it would.

"You need to add yourself, too. You're a true musician," I pointed out.

"I wasn't always that way. I loved the attention even more than Matt."

"You were always better at getting attention, though." Alex smirked at me. He knew I was right.

"Okay, go and find your parents. You'll enjoy showing them around New York. Make sure you're back in time for Shane to get you to the venue, and remember to dress up tonight. I want Steel Roses to go out with a bang." He was so bossy today.

"Alright, I'll see you later." I pecked his lips; it still felt strange not having to hide our relationship.

"See you later. I love you." It felt as if the whole room fell silent as Alex spoke those words. Had nobody else heard him say those words before?

"I love you, too," I beamed before practically skipping off.

It was nice spending a good part of the day with my parents. They'd never been to New York before, which always surprised me as they were so well travelled. My dad was quite the film buff and kept naming movies that had taken place in some of the locations we visited.

The hours passed pretty quickly, and when I looked at my watch I was shocked at the time. We needed to head back soon.

"We're really happy for you, Natty." My dad was smiling at me as I tried to hail down a cab. "Alex will treat you right and look after you."

"I'm not leaving for the moon. You'll still see me, Dad. I haven't abandoned you."

"Oh, I know that. It's just been nice seeing the two of you together."

"That man really loves you," my mother interjected. "I can see it in his eyes when he looks at you."

"I know," I sighed. "I love him, too.... more than I ever thought possible."

"You did good il mio bambino!" My mother hugged me tightly. Why were they acting like they were about to lose me? My parents were so strange at times.

Diego was waiting for me when we got back to the hotel. "What time do you call this?" He was tapping his foot while looking at his watch.

"Come on, I'm only ten minutes late!"

"That's ten minutes less I have to get you ready! Alex gave you orders!" *Jeez, what was with people today?* My parents kissed and hugged me goodbye, and said they'd meet me at the venue later. "Come on, Baby Cakes, we don't have long." Diego hurried me into the elevator.

By the time he had finished, I hardly recognized the girl in the mirror from the person that had applied for the PA job a few years ago. Had I really changed that much? Alex had given me so much, including much needed confidence and a reason to believe in myself.

"You are such a vision. Alex isn't going to be able to control himself when he sees you."

"The dress really is perfect. You're right about the colour."

"It's the Italian in you. Red brings out your features perfectly." I could even walk in three inch heels these days. Diego had taught me well. "Are you ready to go?" There was something different in Diego's eyes. To me, it looked as if he was about to cry at any second. This was Steel Roses last performance for a while, though. Emotions seemed to be high with everyone.

"Yes. Let's do this and then we can finally go home."

"My Ralphie boy will be so happy to see us all!" Diego sighed. "I'll just make sure he doesn't try to hump your leg again."

"It's funnier when he does it to Alex." We were both still chuckling about that as we made our way down to the lobby.

Shane had left a few of his guys so they could escort us to the venue. It was a good job as we looked outside and saw all the paparazzi gathering.

"Are you ready for this?" Diego smirked, handing me some sunglasses to help the glare of the flashing lights.

"I was born ready." Linking my arm in his, we made our way through the crowd and into the waiting car.

Once we arrived at the venue, Diego and I went in search of everyone else. Everyone looked very formal when we did find them. I scanned the crowd, freezing at the sight of David. He was sitting near the front of what seemed to be set up as a press interview room. Had Alex invited him? *What the fuck was going on now? I was done with surprises!*

"Nat," Alex's voice came from behind me. "Wow! You look breathtaking."

"What's going on?" I asked, looking around as some press began to enter the room.

"You're going to love this. Just wait and see." *Ugh! Tell me know, damn it!* He kissed me briefly but deeply. "Take a seat, this won't take long." I sat with Diego and took a further look around. I noticed a few more familiar faces. Milly was here. I was pretty sure Alex's ridiculously rich friend, Oliver Kirkham, who's party Alex performed at last year was here, too, as well as Gina and some guys in suits that I'd never seen before. I had no idea what was going on.

"Thank you for all coming!" Alex took control of the entire room. "I'm sure you're all wondering why I invited you here. For the last ten years, I've been trying to find the right direction for my music. Rock Records has given me so much, but I feel that my time with them is over." *Holy fucking shit! He's leaving Rock Records!?* I wanted to stand up and beg him not to throw his career away, but Diego took my hand in his to soothe me. "Yesterday, Mr. Oliver Kirkham and I set up a new record label that I will be running for him." *What!?* "Harbour Records is hoping to bring new fresh artists to the industry and I'm excited to take on more of a producer role. I'll be leaving Rock Records with immediate effect. Steel Roses might do a few one off shows in the future, but it will be on my terms and without Matt Higgins in the band. Thank you. I'll take a few questions now." Alex was a fucking genius! It was a huge risk to take, but I knew he'd always wanted his own record label where he could release the music he wanted to.

David stood up and stormed out of the room. I couldn't

resist getting up and calling after him. "How does it feel to lose, David?" My face was smug. "Did you and Matt really think you could break us?"

"He's all wrong for you, Nat!" David shouted. "He'll end up destroying you. Why can't you see that?"

"No, *you* were all wrong for me. You never noticed me when I worked for you. I was just a fuck piece you had when you were bored. Alex noticed me the day we met! He's given me so much."

"You go and live in your delusional little world then. I'm done trying to save you! Do you really think he'll stay faithful? He'll drop you within a year."

"I can assure you I won't." Alex wrapped his arms around me from behind. Was the press conference over already? "You never saw Nat for what she was. She is the most beautiful and pure creature I know. I love her more than I can even explain. If you're waiting for her to be single again, you'll have a long wait, motherfucker, because that isn't *ever* happening."

"Fuck the both of you. I'm done!" David looked defeated and I wasn't surprised after Alex's response. There was no way David could have a good comeback after that. "Good luck, Nat." With that he began to walk away.

"Bye, David!" Alex called. "Oh, and don't come looking for a job at Harbour Records because I'll never hire your deceitful, lying, scumbag ass!" Giggling, I looked up at Alex. His eyes were tired but full of love.

"You've been a busy man."

"I wanted to tell you my plan, but I thought this surprise would be better. I didn't finalize the contracts with Oliver until yesterday." That's where he'd been yesterday—with Oliver. "I have one favor to ask you, though."

"What?" I'd give him anything at that moment.

"Will you run Harbour Records with me?" *Oh, my fucking God! White, you just hit the jackpot!* "Is that a yes?" Stunned, I tried to get some words out, but nothing came. "You've been a wonderful PA, but I thought Liv could take that job so you can move on to bigger and better things?"

"I...I'll do it!" I finally managed to force out. Alex crashed his lips against mine in celebration.

"We better get to the stage. Steel Roses are on in half an hour." At least I had no more surprises left; I'm not sure my nerves could have taken anymore.

Alex had the crowd in the palm of his hand as he stood center stage. It was like watching a conductor direct his orchestra; it was beautiful to watch. The band was half way through their setlist, and my heart was getting heavy at the realisation that it was almost over. It was a similar feeling to when I was fifteen and had gone to their concert—that sinking feeling knowing Steel Roses couldn't stay on stage forever, and I didn't know when I'd get to see them live again.

The stage fell silent as a single spotlight illuminated on Alex. This was new. He usually went straight in to Wonderlust at this point.

"New York! How are you feeling?" The crowd roared back. "I want to talk to you about someone that means a lot to me." Fuck! Where was he going with this? "You all now know that I have a girlfriend called Natasha." The audience began to boo me. *Ground swallow me up whole, please!* They all hated me already. "No! No! You shouldn't boo her. Do you want to know why?"

Everyone on the side of the stage was looking at me. What was Alex playing at? "She is one of you. She is the biggest Steel Roses fan ever, and she has the tattoo to prove it." He did not just go there! "Natasha understands what each and every one of you is feeling right now as you watch us perform. She is part of you. If you boo her, you might as well boo yourselves." The crowd went quiet. "I want to invite her onto the stage so you can meet her. Can you promise not to boo her?" The crowd erupted with an almighty cheer. Alex waved me to the stage, but I wasn't fucking moving! I wasn't going to stand in front of over twenty thousand people! Was he insane?! "I think she's scared. Maybe if we all start chanting her name she'll come out." *If I went on that stage right now it would only be to punch him in the chest!*

"Nat, go!" Diego tried to give me a gentle push.

"Don't you fucking dare! That crowd *hates* me!"

"No they don't! Listen...they're chanting your name." Diego was right. The crowd were saying Natasha, Natasha, Natasha over and over again.

Finding all the courage inside me that I could, I slowly began to take small steps towards Alex on the stage. My heart felt as if it was hammering outside my chest. Once I reached him, I calmed a little, but was startled at the happy cheer from the crowd below me. Holy fuck! I was on stage with Steel Roses in front of twenty thousand people! *Keep it cool, White!*

"Here she is," Alex announced, making them go even crazier. "I'm going to sing a song that was inspired by this beautiful woman." Stage crew suddenly appeared with a stool that I could sit on. "You'll all know this one well. It's called Wonderlust." How would I keep my cool with Alex singing to me on stage?

I'd lost track of the number of times I'd heard Alex sing Wonderlust, but this was different. Not once did he take his eyes off me as he sang. Each word that came from his lips had a new meaning, and I couldn't help the happy tears that trickled down my face. Diego was going to kill me, as I was pretty sure I'd ruined my makeup.

Alex came to the last few words of the song and got down on one knee. Taking my hand in his he sang the last line *'I'm feeling wonderlust baby, pure wonderlust.'* I could hardly see through my happy tears. "I have one more thing to do while I'm kneeling on the floor." Alex placed his mic on the ground and reached into his pocket. I stopped breathing in that instant. *Breathe, Nat, Fucking breathe!*

He pulled out a small red box and I gasped. He wasn't serious, was he? Here? Now? This crowd was about to lynch me!

Alex spoke, but I could hardly hear him. The audience was going crazy. "Natasha White, you're crazy ass completes me. I don't want to spend the rest of my life with anyone but you. Will you make me the happiest man in the world by agreeing to marry me?" Slowly, he opened the ring box. Inside was the most beautiful cluster diamond ring I had ever seen. Swallowing hard, I wiped the tears that had trickled down my face. We hadn't even spoken about marriage! I didn't think Alex was the marrying type. Did I *want* to marry him? *Stupid question! Of course I did!*

It was such a big step—giving yourself completely to someone—but the more I thought about it, I realized I'd already given myself to Alex. With that realization, I knew I was ready for this.

Kneeling down on the stage in front of Alex, I took his face in my hands. He was hanging on my answer.

"Yes! Yes, yes, yes! Of course I'll marry you," I sobbed. His lips crashed furiously against mine and I was lost in him. I was going to be Mrs. Harbour, and I could hardly wait!

"She said yes!" Alex yelled at the crowd after our lips parted. The noise was deafening as everyone jumped up and down, celebrating with us. "Meet the future Mrs. Harbour!" I took a little bow, then Alex let me go back to the side of the stage.

Everyone was waiting to congratulate me. "You knew, didn't you?" They all looked sheepish. Alex had planned *everything.* This was why he'd flown my parents here. Had he asked my dad's permission for my hand in marriage? *I bet he had!* That was why my parents had been acting weird earlier. He'd even made sure the fans would be on my side because I was one of them. Alex had basically protected me in every way that he could. I stood watching the rest of the show in utter wonderment at how much he'd done for me.

The concert came to an end and Steel Roses took their final bow. Just like that, the tour was over. Matt was the first to storm off. He didn't speak to a single soul as he barged past everyone. I had a feeling that was the last we would see of him.

Alex found me in the crowd and rushed over, picking me up and swinging me around. "I think it's time to celebrate!"

"I can't believe you planned all this!"

"I wanted to surprise you."

"Well, you definitely did that," I snorted, looking around at all our closest friends and family. "And you lot were in on it!"

"Don't be so hard on them. We all know you hate surprises, but it had to be done."

"I'm waiting to see what happens next. You're full of surprises today." Wrapping my arms around his neck, I pulled him closer towards me.

"No, no more surprises. Now we go home, plan a wedding, and live our lives." I had to admit that sounded perfect. "We might even have time for stargazing, too," he muttered, looking down at my mouth. As his lips pressed against mine, all my fear and concern evaporated. Okay, I was going to marry *Alex Harbour, Legendary Sex God,* but that didn't mean we were doomed. Love was what made our world go around, and Alex and I had that in abundance. We had a new record label that would finally take him in the direction he wanted, and a wedding to plan that would blind us forever.

Life with my rock star was just beginning, and I, for one, couldn't wait to see the amazing life we were going to give each other.

EPILOGUE

A lex had been gone for hours. I thought we were done with surprises now that we were back home in LA. Apparently there was one left, but he had to go and collect it. How much more I could take? I was on a constant high, knowing that I was Alex Harbour's fiancée. What more could he possibly surprise me with? Surely nothing would top his wedding proposal.

"Nat, do you want anything to eat?" Mary called over to me. I was currently sitting by the pool, enjoying the midday sun.

"No, I'll wait until Alex gets home. Thanks, though." Coming back to Alex's Hollywood mansion really felt like coming home, but then I guess this *was* my home now. We were getting married, after all. Alex wanted to take me away for a romantic break next week. Truthfully I just wanted to hide away in our home for a little while. The year on the road with Steel Roses had definitely taken its toll on my enjoyment of staying in hotels. If I ever saw a room service menu again, it would be too soon. It wasn't that I didn't want to travel with him, I just wanted a bit of routine here first.

Harbour Records was starting to take shape. Alex was meeting with Central Demons next week to get them signed to the label. Lance was excited to be working with us. He'd idolized Alex when he helped them get signed at Rock Records. Sadly, they were dropped by no fault of their own. Rock Records took them in the wrong direction. Alex knew exactly what sound and image they needed to get noticed. It was going to be exciting watching the company grow. With Oliver Kirkham being our silent sponsor, we had a lot of equity in the business already. The goal was to pay Oliver back once the company was earning enough. Alex had a five year plan to achieve this.

"Look at you glowing in the sunshine." Alex's voice came from behind me. Snapping around to gaze at him, I couldn't help but wonder if he had the surprise with him. I froze. Had Alex gotten a new tattoo on his wrist? It was wrapped up like he had.

"Did you get another tattoo?" I frowned, putting my hand up to shield the sun from my eyes.

"This is your surprise." Now I was confused. How could him getting a new tattoo be a surprise for *me*? "Come into my music room for a moment. The lighting is better in there." Following him wordlessly, I tried to wrack my brain about the type of tattoo he might have had done. He hadn't mentioned anything to me while we'd been on tour, though.

"It's almost finished. It just needs a bit more work on the words." He began to unwrap his right wrist from the plastic wrap that was protecting it. He'd gotten another word tattoo? Now I was intrigued. "I wanted something that symbolizes the point I'm at in my life right now...something that shows the man I was, but also the man I've become because of you." I wasn't sure if I was able to take a breath, too fixated on his wrist as he finally revealed it to me. My eyes widened as I looked at the inside of his right wrist. There, tattooed forever in ink, was a star constellation. Not just any, though; it was *Orion*, the first constellation I found with my dad when I was a child. It always reminded me of home because it could be seen anywhere in the world. Everyone knew the name of Orion because it was the most well-known. You could almost say the star system was famous. It was perfect for Alex. Looking closer, I noticed the wording. It was in latin, like his other one. "All of this symbolizes you, Straight Lace. You're permanently inked on my skin, just like you are with my heart." A single tear trickled down my face at his confession. "It took me a while to decide on the words, though." *Per aspera ad astra* was written below the constellation. My latin wasn't very good, but I knew those words had to be about me. "It means 'through hardships to the stars.' You *are* my star, Nat. You made me defeat my demons and I'll never be able to repay you for that." I couldn't form a single sentence; Alex had rendered me speechless. I meant *that* much to him? Had I really saved him?

All I could do was crash my lips fiercely against his, pouring all my love and admiration into the kiss. The fresh ink on his skin had tethered us forever. Alex had me—heart, body and soul. I would always be his star that would guide him home.

ABOUT THE AUTHOR

B. L. Wilde

Visit www.blwilde.com for more news

BOOKS BY THIS AUTHOR

The Seductors Series

The Human Mating Site

Printed in Great Britain
by Amazon

36984706R20138